A Winning Spirit

A Molly Classic
Volume 1

by Valerie Tripp

★ AmericanGirl®

Published by American Girl Publishing

18 19 20 21 22 23 QP 11 10 9 8 7 6 5 4 3 2

Cover image by David Roth and Juliana Kolesova

Cataloging-in-Publication Data available from the Library of Congress

To my family

To all my teachers

To Michael

Beforever™

The adventurous characters you'll meet in
the BeForever books will spark your curiosity
about the past, inspire you to find your voice
in the present, and excite you about your future.
You'll make friends with these girls as you share
their fun and their challenges. Like you, they are
bright and brave, imaginative and energetic,
creative and kind. Just as you are, they are
discovering what really matters: Helping others.
Being a true friend. Protecting the earth.
Standing up for what's right. Read their stories,
explore their worlds, join their adventures.
Your friendship with them will BeForever.

TABLE *of* CONTENTS

Turnips

✪ CHAPTER 1 ✪

olly McIntire sat at the kitchen table day-
dreaming about her Halloween costume. It
would be a pink dress with a long, floaty
skirt that would swirl when she turned and swish
when she walked. There would be shiny silver stars
on the skirt to match the stars in her crown. The top of
the dress would be white. Maybe it would be made of
fluffy angora, only Molly wasn't sure they had angora
back in Cinderella's time. That's who Molly wanted to
be for Halloween—Cinderella. All she had to do was

1. talk her mother into buying the material and
   making the costume,
2. find some glass slippers somewhere, and
3. convince Linda and Susan, her two best friends,
   to be the ugly stepsisters.

She could probably talk Susan into it. As long as

Susan got to wear a long dress, she wouldn't mind being a stepsister. But Linda was another story. If they were going to be fairy-tale princesses, Linda would want to be Snow White because she had black hair just like Snow White's. Linda would want Molly and Susan to be dwarfs. *Probably Sleepy and Grumpy,* thought Molly.

Well, Molly certainly felt like Grumpy tonight. She looked at the clock. She had been sitting at the kitchen table for exactly two hours, forty-six minutes, and one, two, three seconds. She had been sitting at the kitchen table, in fact, ever since six o'clock, when Mrs. Gilford, the housekeeper, called everyone to supper.

Molly had smelled trouble as soon as she walked into the kitchen. It was a heavy, hot smell, kind of like the smell of dirty socks. She sat down and saw the odd orange heap on her plate. She made up her mind right away not to eat it. "What's this orange stuff?" she asked.

Mrs. Gilford turned around and gave her what Molly's father used to call the Gladys Gilford Glacial Glare. "Polite children do not refer to food as *stuff*," said Mrs. Gilford. "The vegetable which you are lucky enough to have on your plate is mashed turnip."

"I'd like to *re*turn it," whispered Molly's twelve-year-old brother Ricky.

"What was that, young man?" asked Mrs. Gilford sharply.

"I like to *eat* turnips," said Ricky, and he shoveled a forkful into his mouth. Eating turnips—or anything alive or dead—was no hardship for Ricky. If it could be chewed, Ricky would eat it. Quick as a wink, all his turnips were gone.

That rat Ricky, thought Molly. She looked over at her older sister, Jill. Jill was putting ladylike bites of turnip in her mouth and washing them down with long, quiet sips of water. Almost all of the horrible orange stuff was gone from her plate.

Molly sighed. In the old days, before Jill turned fourteen and got stuck-up, Molly used to be able to count on her to make a big fuss about things like turnips. But lately, Molly had to do it all herself. Jill was acting superior. This new grown-up Jill was a terrible disappointment to Molly. If that's what happened to you when you got to be fourteen, Molly would rather be nine forever.

The turnips sat on Molly's plate getting cold. They were turning into a solid lump that oozed water. With her fork, Molly carefully pushed her meat and potatoes to a corner of her plate so that not a speck of turnip would touch them and ruin them. "Disgusting," she said softly.

"There will be no such language used at this table," said Mrs. Gilford. "Furthermore, anyone who fails to finish her turnips will have no dessert. Nor will she be allowed to leave the table until the turnips are gone."

That's why Molly was still at the kitchen table facing a plate of cold turnips at 8:46 P.M. *None of this would have happened if Dad were home,* she thought. Molly touched the heart-shaped locket she wore on a thin chain around her neck. She pulled it forward and opened it up to look at the tiny picture inside. Her father's face smiled back at her.

Molly's father was a doctor. When American soldiers started fighting in World War Two, he joined the Army. Now he was somewhere in England, taking care of wounded and sick soldiers. He had been gone for seven months. Molly missed him every single minute of every single day, but especially at dinnertime.

Before Dad left, before the war, Molly's family never ate supper in the kitchen. They ate dinner in the dining room. Before Dad left, back before the war, the whole family always had dinner together. They laughed and talked the whole time. Now things were different. Dad was gone, and every morning Molly's mother went off to work at the Red Cross headquarters. Very often she got home too late to have dinner with the family. And she spent at least an hour every night writing to Dad.

When a letter came from Dad, it was a surprise and a treat. Everyone gathered and listened in silence while Mrs. McIntire read the letter aloud. Dad always sent a special message to each member of the family. He told jokes and drew funny sketches of himself. But he didn't say which hospital he worked in or name any of the towns he visited. That wasn't allowed, because of the war. And even though Dad's letters were long and funny and wonderful, they still sounded as if they came from very far away. They were not at all like the words Dad spoke in his deep-down voice that you could feel rumbling inside you and filling up the house. Molly used to be able to hear that voice even when she was up in her room doing homework.

When Dad called out, "I'm home!" the house seemed more lively. Everyone, even Jill, would tumble down the stairs for a big hug. Then Dad would sit in his old plaid chair, cozy in a warm circle of lamplight, and they'd tell him what had gone on in school that day. Dad's pipe smoke made the room smell of vanilla and burning leaves. Sometimes, now that Dad was gone to the war, Molly would climb into the plaid chair and sniff it because that vanilla pipe smell made her feel so safe and happy, just as if Dad were home.

Molly remembered the fun they had at the dinner table when Dad was home. He teased Jill and made her blush. He swapped jokes with Ricky and told riddles to Brad, Molly's younger brother. And he always said, "Gosh and golly, olly Molly, what have *you* done to-day?" Suddenly, everything Molly had done—whether it was winning a running race or losing a multiplica-tion bee—was interesting and important, wonderful or not so bad after all.

Dad loved to tease Mrs. Gilford, too. As she carried steaming trays out from the kitchen with lots of importance, Dad would say, "Mrs. Gladys Gilford,

an advancement has been made tonight in the art
of cooking. Never before in the history of mankind
has there been such a perfect pot roast." Mrs. Gilford
would beam and bustle and serve up more perfect pot
roast and mashed potatoes and gravy. She never, ever,
served anything awful like turnips.

But everything was different now because of the
war. Dad was gone and Mom was busy at the Red
Cross. So Mrs. Gilford, who had arrived at the dot of
seven o'clock every weekday morning of Molly's life
to cook and clean, now ruled the roost more than ever.
And Mrs. Gilford was determined to do her part to
help win the war.

A Victory garden was Mrs. Gilford's latest war
effort. Last spring she sent away for a pamphlet called
Food Fights for Freedom. It explained how to start a Victory garden in your own backyard. The pamphlet had
a picture of vegetables lined up in front of a potato and
an onion that were wearing military hats and saluting.
Under the picture it said, "Call vegetables into service."

"From now on, there will be no more canned vegetables used in this house," Mrs. Gilford announced.
"The soldiers need the tin in those cans more than we

do. From now on, we will grow, preserve, and eat our own vegetables. It's the least we can do for our fighting boys."

All summer long, Mrs. Gilford had tended her Victory garden. She wore a stiff straw hat, Dr. McIntire's gardening gloves, and knee-high black rubber boots. Everyone, even little Brad, had helped her. Molly had worked in the Victory garden every Tuesday morning from ten to eleven o'clock. She had crawled on her hands and knees through rows of green seedlings, pulling weeds. The rows were as strict and straight as soldiers on parade. Each one was labeled with a colorful seed packet on a stake. The seed packets showed fat carrots, plump red tomatoes, and big green peas.

But by fall, after months in the hot sun, the pictures on the seed packets had faded away. The packets hung on the stakes like limp white flags of surrender. Mrs. Gilford's Victory garden had not been quite as victorious as she had hoped. All but the toughest vegetables had been beaten by the dry summer. The carrots were thin and wrinkled. The tomatoes were as hard as nuts. The peas were brown. But that did not defeat Mrs. Gilford. She would never give up and open a tin can. She had a rather successful crop of radishes, lima beans, and turnips, so that's what they would eat.

As Molly stared at the turnips on her plate, she remembered Mrs. Gilford saying, "Wasting food is not only childish and selfish, it is unpatriotic. Think of your poor father off in some strange land. Maybe he didn't have enough to eat tonight. And you turn up your nose at fresh turnips. You will not leave this table until those turnips are gone. Completely."

Now it was almost nine o'clock. It was getting cold in the kitchen. Molly was lonely. She was tired of thinking about how unpatriotic she was. She looked at the turnips, lifted a tiny forkful, and put it in her mouth. Just then Ricky burst through the swinging kitchen door.

"How do you like eating old, cold, moldy brains?" he teased. Then he ran out.

Molly swallowed the turnips fast, then gulped down a whole glass of water. Old, cold, moldy brains was exactly what the turnips were like. She would not eat one speck more.

"Ricky, you rat!" she said. "I'm going to get you!" She started to get up from the chair.

From behind the door Ricky chanted, "Nyah, nyah, nyah-nyah nyah! You can't leave the table. You haven't finished your turnips!"

"Ricky, stop it!" yelled Molly. But Ricky was right. The turnips were still on her plate, and she was stuck. To make matters worse, Molly heard her mother calling good-bye to the car-sharing group she rode with from Red Cross headquarters.

Now Mom will be mad at me, too, thought Molly. *Now she'll never make a Cinderella dress for my Halloween costume. Now everyone in the house will be mad at me for making Mom upset. And all because of these terrible turnips.*

Mrs. McIntire walked in the back door, looked at Molly, looked at the plate, and knew immediately what had happened. "Well, Molly," she said. "I see we had the first turnips from the Victory garden for dinner tonight."

"Mom," said Molly, "I hate turnips. I know I do. And Mrs. Gilford says I can't leave the table until I eat them. I'll be here until I die, because I will never eat these. Never. I really mean it."

"I see," said Molly's mother. "Do you mind if I join you for a while? Not until you die, of course—just

☆ Turnips ☆

while I have a cup of tea. And while I'm heating up the stove, why don't I reheat those turnips for you? They certainly don't look very good when they're cold like that."

"It won't help," said Molly.

But Mrs. McIntire scooped up the turnips and put them in a frying pan. "I'll just smooth out these lumps. And I think we can spare a little bit of our sugar and butter rations to add to the turnips," she said, almost to herself. "And a little cinnamon, too."

Soon a delicious, spicy aroma filled the kitchen. The kettle whistled, and Mrs. McIntire made her tea. She spooned the turnips back onto Molly's plate and put the plate in front of Molly.

The hot steam from the turnips warmed Molly's face and clouded her glasses. She took a deep breath, raised a small forkful to her lips, and tasted it. It wasn't so bad. In fact, it was pretty good—sweet, cinnamony, and kind of like applesauce. It felt good going down, not at all like old, cold, moldy brains. She ate another forkful.

Mrs. McIntire sat down with her tea. "When I was about your age," she said, "my mother made sardines on toast for dinner one night. Little oily dead fish on toast! I refused to eat them. But my mother said I could not leave the table until the sardines were gone. Gone was exactly what she said. So when she wasn't looking I put each sardine, one by one, into my napkin. Then I stuck my napkin into my pocket. When my mother saw my empty plate she was surprised, but she excused me from the table.

"I used to play checkers with my father every night after dinner. That night it was very hard to concentrate on the game. Our two cats, Bessy and May, yowled and meowed and climbed all over me. They smelled the sardines. Finally, when I had one hand on Bessy and the other hand on a checker, May pulled the napkin out of my pocket. The sardines spilled out all over the rug. Bessy and May gobbled them up."

"Oh, Mom!" laughed Molly.

"Oh, Molly," sighed Mrs. McIntire. "Sometimes we have to do things whether we like it or not. There aren't always cats around who will eat the sardines." She reached across the table and brushed Molly's bangs out of her eyes. "I know this war is hard on you children. And I know you miss your father. I miss him, too."

"Everything is so different with Dad gone," said Molly. "Nothing is the way it used to be anymore."

"The war has changed things," said Mrs. McIntire. "But some things are still the same. Isn't Ricky still Ricky?"

"He sure is," said Molly. "Still dumb old Ricky."

"And you are still my olly Molly," Mrs. McIntire said. "And I am still me." She gave Molly's hand a squeeze.

Molly smiled. The turnips were gone. Mom was not mad. Mrs. Gilford wouldn't think that Molly was ruining her war effort.

"Thanks, Mom," she said as she gave her mother a hug. Molly walked carefully up the stairs to bed, pretending she was wearing a long, floaty pink skirt that swished as she took each step.

Hula Dancers

✪ CHAPTER 2 ✪

he next morning dawned all gold and blue and windy. *This is perfect Halloween weather,* Molly thought as she woke up. At breakfast Mrs. Gilford didn't say anything about the turnips, but she made French toast, which was a sign that all was forgiven.

It was Thursday, and Molly's friends Linda and Susan were coming home with her after school. They were going to plan their Halloween costumes. They had made a secret pact not to discuss their ideas until they got to Molly's house. "Someone might copy us if they heard our idea," said Molly. Linda and Susan agreed. Besides, it was fun to have a secret pact—it was sort of like being soldiers and keeping battle plans away from enemy spies.

As they walked home after school, they met Alison

Hargate, who was one of their classmates. She asked, "What are you three going to be for Halloween?"

"We can't tell," said Molly. "It's a surprise."

"Oh," said Alison.

Linda said, "But it's *great*. It's really a great idea."

Susan chimed in, "Yes! It's wonderful! We're going to have the best Halloween costumes ever."

Alison looked impressed. Molly was a little worried. The girls hadn't even agreed on what they were going to be. The mystery was making their costumes get a lot of attention. They were really going to have to make good costumes, or everyone would tease them.

"What are you going to be, Alison?" Molly asked.

"Oh, probably an angel," said Alison. "My mother said I could wear her white satin dressing gown, and she's already made me some gold wings and a halo."

Molly, Linda, and Susan were suddenly very quiet. Molly was jealous. She was sorry she had even asked Alison. An angel! What a great idea! Alison was sure to look wonderful with a halo over her golden hair.

It was hard to have Alison for a friend. Alison was an only child, and her parents were rich and gave her everything that anyone could want. Alison didn't mean to brag about the things she had, but just by telling the truth she managed to make everyone resent her.

"My mother doesn't even have a dressing gown, much less a white satin one," said Linda glumly. "All she has is a brown terry cloth bathrobe. I know she'd never even let me wear that."

"Well," said Molly to Alison, "all I can tell you is that *our* idea is much more . . . um . . . original than an angel."

"Yeah, I know an angel is kind of boring," said Alison quickly. "It was my mother's idea. She made the wings and all."

"Well, see you later, Alison," said Molly as she and Linda and Susan hurried away. It made them uncomfortable when Alison started being so *nice*.

When the girls got to Molly's house, they went into the kitchen for a snack.

"Hello, Mrs. Gilford," they said together.

"Hello, girls," answered Mrs. Gilford. "There are some apples in the bowl on the table. Help yourselves, but take your apples outside, please. It's too nice a day to be cooped up in the house."

"Thank you, Mrs. Gilford," the girls said as they

went to sit on the back steps in the sunshine. Ricky was out back, too, shooting baskets at the hoop on the side of the garage. He was trying to set a world record for making the most baskets without missing.

As the girls munched their apples, Susan said, "Gee, I think an angel is a good idea. Why don't we be angels, too?"

"Absolutely not," said Molly. "Do you want Alison to think we stole her idea?"

"Alison wouldn't mind," said Susan.

"I know," said Molly. "But *I* would mind. We can think of something just as good."

"Like what?" asked Linda.

"Well," replied Molly slowly, as if she had just thought of it for the very first time. "How about Cinderella and the two ug—I mean, the two step-sisters?"

"Oooooh," said Susan. "Cinderella!"

"Who gets to be Cinderella?" Linda asked.

"We don't have to decide that right away," said Molly. "Let's . . . uh . . . let's wait and see who has the best ball dress, and that's the one who will be Cinder-ella. The other two will be stepsisters."

"I don't think it's fair," Linda stated. "Who wants to be an ugly stepsister?"

"You're all ugly step *sitters* today," teased Ricky. "Get it?"

"Cut it out, Ricky," said Molly. Ricky went back to shooting baskets.

"I think it's a good idea," said Susan. "My sister Gloria just gave me an old prom dress of hers. It's sort of green, with a big petticoat and shiny gold threads at the bottom of the skirt. I'll wear that."

"Sort of green," Ricky mocked. "Lima bean green is what you mean."

"Ricky, go away," said Molly. But she was thinking that Susan's dress sounded perfect for Cinderella. And it had two very big advantages over Molly's floaty pink dress with the white angora top. Susan's dress really existed, and Susan already had it. Being an ugly stepsister was not at all what Molly had in mind.

"Wait a minute," she said. "Maybe Linda is right. Maybe it's not fair. Maybe we should all be exactly the same thing, like the Three Musketeers."

"You'd be perfect as the Three Little Pigs," said Ricky. "Or you could be the Three Bears. How about the Three Stooges? Or the Three Kings of Orient?" He began to sing in a loud, teasing voice:

> We three kings of Orient are,
> Tried to smoke a rubber cigar,
> It was loaded, it exploded . . .

"STOP IT!" yelled Molly.

And suddenly, Ricky did stop. His face turned red. He bounced the basketball under his legs, then behind his back. He leaned casually against the garage and twirled the ball on the tip of one finger.

The girls turned around to see who he was showing off for. It wasn't Mrs. Gilford or even Mrs. McIntire. Nobody was there except Jill and her new best friend Dolores. They were walking up the driveway, carrying their school books.

Dolores was wearing a bright blue sweater just the color of her eyes. She had a wide, white smile, like a movie star in a toothpaste ad. She stopped and flashed her smile at Ricky.

"Hi, Rich," she said.

"Rich!" snorted Molly. Lately, Ricky had been

telling everybody to call him Rich because it sounded more like a soldier's name than Ricky did.

"Hi, Dolores," he squeaked in a very odd voice. He turned quickly, jumped, and sent the basketball swishing through the basket just as Dolores went in the door.

Molly, Linda, and Susan looked at one another and dissolved into giggles. It was crystal clear to them what Ricky's problem was. Ricky-Rich had a crush on Dolores! The three girls started to chant:

> *Ricky and Dolores up in a tree,*
> *K-I-S-S-I-N-G!*
> *First comes love,*
> *Then comes marriage,*
> *Then comes Ricky with a baby carriage!*

Ricky threw the basketball at the girls, but they hopped up and out of the way. Then they started making loud, slurpy kissing noises. "Ricky has a crush!" they chanted. "Ricky loves Dolores!"

"Hi-i-i, Do-lor-esss," Molly squeaked, imitating Ricky. She pretended to kiss the basketball.

"Eeeeeuuuuwwww!" Linda and Susan shrieked.

Ricky jumped on his bike. As he sped past the girls he called, "You'll be sorry! You'll *pay* for this!"

The girls just giggled until they ran out of breath and their stomachs hurt. Finally, they got serious again and went back to the question of what to be for Halloween.

"We could be the princesses of England," suggested Linda.

"But there are only two of them, Elizabeth and Margaret Rose. One of us would have to be their mother," said Molly.

"How about being nurses?" asked Susan. "We could all wear capes."

"That's what we did *last* year!" Linda and Molly said together.

They considered being acrobats, three Alices in Wonderland, ice skating stars like Sonja Henie, or the Three Blind Mice. No one could get very excited about being a blind mouse, and anyway, Mrs. McIntire overheard them and said she absolutely did not have time to make a mouse costume for Molly. "And besides," added Mrs. McIntire, "in wartime I don't think it's right to use good material for Halloween costumes."

Molly, Linda, and Susan groaned. They knew Mrs. McIntire was right.

"But I've got another idea," said Mrs. McIntire. "I'll show you girls how to make grass skirts out of newspaper and crepe paper. Then you can be hula dancers."

"Well," replied Susan, "my sister Gloria taught me how to make flowers out of crepe paper, just like they did to decorate for the prom. We could string them together and make flower necklaces and headdresses."

"I think my father has an old ukulele," said Linda. "It doesn't have any strings, but it will look good."

"It's too bad it's so cold, because I know my mother will make me wear socks and shoes and a sweater on top," said Susan. "But at least the flower necklaces will hide most of the sweater."

So the girls decided to be Hawaiian hula dancers for Halloween.

Soon after that, the streetlights went on, which meant Linda and Susan had to go home. They agreed to meet back at Molly's house after school the next afternoon to make their costumes. Then they would all go trick-or-treating together. Afterward, Linda and

Susan would spend the night at Molly's so they could talk about how wonderful their Halloween had been.

By the time she went inside to supper, Molly had completely forgotten Ricky's threat to make them all sorry. She was too busy practicing her hula.

Trick or Treat?

 he grass skirt made out of newspaper and crepe paper was not exactly as glamorous as the pink floaty skirt Molly had imagined. But it was quite long, and it did make a nice rustling noise as she walked. Besides, making the skirts had been lots of fun. Mom came home from Red Cross headquarters early, just so she could help. She put on a record of Hawaiian songs. Then they all sat in the den, cutting the newspaper into strips. They covered the newspaper with strips of green crepe paper. Mom sewed all the paper strips onto long pieces of cloth to tie around their waists like aprons. Susan showed them how to make crepe paper flowers that were big and colorful. They made strings of the paper flowers to use as necklaces and bracelets. Mrs. McIntire even squirted some of her perfume on them.

By the time they were ready to go out trick-or-treating, Molly, Linda, and Susan were caught up in the excitement of Halloween and very pleased with their matching hula outfits.

"Adorable!" said Dolores. "You look as cute as buttons!" She and Jill bobby-pinned paper flowers into the girls' hair.

"When I get back from taking Brad trick-or-treating, I'll take your picture to send to Dad," said Mrs. McIntire. Brad was wearing a sheet. He was going as a ghost. "Ricky, I'll want a picture of you, too."

"Okay, Mom," said Ricky. He was dressed as a pirate. Ricky was a pirate every year.

It was a windy night, but not too cold, so the girls rolled down their socks and pushed up the sleeves of their sweaters. The wind made their skirts ripple so that they looked graceful and pretty, just like real grass skirts.

They saw Alison when they went to the Silvanos' house down the street. Her angel outfit was perfect. She had a flowing white satin robe with fluffy white feathers at the neck and cuffs and all down the front. Her wings and halo were covered with gold glitter.

"Hula dancers!" Alison sighed with envy when she saw them.

Molly was very pleased. *They* had made Alison jealous. "Your outfit is good, too," Molly said. "You really look like an angel." She felt like being nice. In fact, it would probably be fun to trick-or-treat with Alison, except Alison's mother always went with her.

"Hawaiian hula dancers!" Mrs. Hargate was saying. "What charming costumes, gals! And homemade, too! Aren't you clever?" The girls just smiled and hurried away.

"Really," Linda said later, "you almost have to feel sorry for Alison with a mother like that!"

"I know," said Molly. "Wouldn't it be awful to have a mother who doesn't know that the whole *point* of Halloween is to go out and walk around the neighborhood with your friends, and not with her?"

Because of the war, most people did not have any sugar to spare, so the girls did not get as many candies and cookies as last year. Nevertheless, their brown paper bags were soon bulging with apples, peanuts, and homemade doughnuts, molasses kisses, and popcorn balls. The Hargates' maid was giving out Tootsie

Pops, which were the best treats.

Two families, the Pedersons and the Rucksteins, asked the girls to do a trick before they got their treats. So the girls did a hula, waving their arms and singing the Hawaiian song they learned in school. Linda strummed her stringless ukulele. It was a big hit. The Pedersons, especially, clapped and clapped. They gave the girls each two glasses of cider.

Linda believed in eating her treats along the way, so her bag was not as full as Susan's and Molly's when the girls finally walked up the driveway to Molly's house. Molly was humming the Hawaiian song, Linda was unwrapping a popcorn ball, and Susan was making her skirt swish and sway. They were almost to the back door when a huge splash of water poured down on top of them and a hose sprayed straight at them.

"AHHHH!" Molly yelled. The water flooded around her feet in cold gushes. She felt as if she was drowning in a waterfall. Her bag of treats burst, the popcorn balls floated in puddles, the doughnuts turned to spongy globs, the apples rolled away down the sidewalk. Linda and Susan were gasping. Their paper flowers were flattened. Their skirts were hanging in shreds. The green dye from the crepe paper was dripping down their legs onto their socks.

When the water finally stopped, Molly's hair was stuck to her forehead, her hands were full of melting paper flowers, and most of her hula skirt lay in soggy ribbons in the driveway.

"Ruined! Wrecked! Completely wrecked!" sobbed Molly. "Who would play such a mean trick?"

Then the girls heard Ricky singing in a low, slow, steady voice:

> *I see London,*
> *I see France,*
> *I can see your underpants!*

"Ricky," yowled Molly, "I'll get you for this! You ruined everything! You'll be sorry—you wait! You'll be *really* sorry."

Ricky threw the hose down and ran off. The girls just stood there in the driveway, stunned with surprise and sputtering with anger. Maybe they shouldn't have teased Ricky about Dolores, but who ever would have expected him to get back at them in such a mean way?

Finally Linda said, "I'm freezing!"

Molly said, "You two go on inside. I'll clean up this mess. Then we've got some planning to do. We have to teach Ricky a lesson he'll never forget."

War!

❂ CHAPTER 4 ❂

while later, Linda, Susan, and Molly sat in Molly's room in their pajamas. Still pink from their baths, wrapped head to toe in big white blankets, they looked like three rosy polar bears. The girls were whispering together on Molly's bed when they heard Mrs. McIntire returning with Brad.

"Would you hula dancers like some cocoa?" Mrs. McIntire called up to the girls.

"Okay, Mom," called Molly. "We'll be right down."

"Good!" said Susan. "Now we can tell her what Ricky did!"

"No!" Molly said quickly.

"Why not?" asked Susan.

"I don't want to be a tattletale," said Molly. "And besides, Mom would be too easy on him. We just have to take care of Ricky ourselves."

The girls walked slowly into the kitchen. There at the table sat Ricky, still in his pirate costume. He was sipping cocoa and looking as innocent as a kitten. Molly, Linda, and Susan sat as far away from Ricky as possible.

"Well, girls," said Mrs. McIntire. "How was your Hawaiian Halloween?"

"Fine," said the three girls all together, but it sounded as if they meant just the opposite.

Mrs. McIntire looked puzzled. "Just 'fine'? That's all?" she asked. "And why are you all in your pajamas already? I wanted to take your picture to send to Dad. What happened to your costumes? And your treats?"

"They got wet," said Molly.

"Wet?" asked Mrs. McIntire. "How?"

The girls looked at each other. "By a hose," said Susan. "Ricky—"

"We walked into a hose. By mistake," said Molly quickly, before Susan could finish.

"Who would be using a hose on a windy Halloween night?" asked Mrs. McIntire.

The girls said nothing. Finally Molly said, "Just someone."

Mrs. McIntire frowned. "Molly McIntire," she said. "I have the distinct feeling that I am not being told the whole story."

Molly stared into her cocoa cup. Ricky pushed his chair back from the table.

"Perhaps *you* can tell me what happened, Ricky," said Mrs. McIntire.

"Me?" squeaked Ricky. He fiddled with the handle of his pirate dagger. "I didn't . . . I mean . . . I mean . . ."

"Go on, Ricky," said Mrs. McIntire.

"Well, it was just a joke, Mom," said Ricky. "Just a joke on the girls. You know, a Halloween joke? Trick or treat?"

"A *mean* trick," muttered Linda.

"What did you do?" asked Mrs. McIntire, staring steadily at Ricky.

"I just got a little water on their costumes," he said.

"A *little* water?" squealed Molly. "You dumped pails and pails of water all over us, Ricky!"

"You squirted us with a *hose!*" Susan added.

"You ruined our costumes and all our treats!" said Linda.

"Is that true?" asked Mrs. McIntire.

"Yes!" exclaimed all the girls.

"Ricky?"

"Yes, ma'am," muttered Ricky. He looked down at his feet.

Mrs. McIntire was quiet. Then she said, "Ricky, that was a very mean thing to do. I'm ashamed of you, treating your sister and her friends that way. I think I can say that your father would be ashamed of you, too. I'm going to punish you just as I think he would punish you." Mrs. McIntire sighed. "You are to apologize to these girls. Then you are to give your bag of Halloween treats to Linda, Susan, and Molly to share. You may keep one treat, and only one, for yourself. I'm going upstairs to put Brad to bed now, and while I'm gone I want you to apologize. Is that clear?"

"Yes, ma'am," said Ricky.

"Girls, after Ricky apologizes, I want you to go to bed. I'll come in later to say good night," said Mrs. McIntire as she left with Brad.

After she had gone, Ricky muttered, "Sorry." Then he shoved his bag of Halloween treats into Molly's hand and ran out of the kitchen.

As the girls trudged up to bed, Linda whispered,

"You were right, Molly. She was way too easy on him."

"Yeah!" said Susan. "Except for the part about your father being ashamed."

"He wrecked our Halloween, and he's hardly suffering at all!" added Linda.

"Well," said Molly as she flopped on her bed, "we'll just have to think up a plan to make Ricky *really* suffer."

"Let's let the air out of his bicycle tires," suggested Susan.

"Not bad enough," said Molly.

"We could put frogs under his pillow," said Linda. "Dozens and dozens of frogs."

"Yeah, but then we'd have to catch the frogs," Susan pointed out.

"Eeeeeuuuuwwww!" they all shrieked.

"We could disguise our voices and call him up on the telephone," said Susan. "We could pretend we're Mrs. Mobley, his teacher, and say he has to stay after school every day next week for being bad."

"No," said Molly. "That's no good. It doesn't embarrass him in front of anybody. We have to really embarrass him in front of lots of people, or in front of someone he'd hate to be embarrassed in front of, like Mom, or . . ."

"Or Dolores!" said Linda.

"Yes, that's it!" said Molly. "Embarrass him in front of Dolores!"

"But how?" asked Susan.

The girls were quiet for a minute. Molly was still mad—as mad as a wet hen, her father would say. She could remember Ricky chanting, "I see London, I see France, I can see your underpants."

Underpants? Dolores? Molly thought. Then she smiled to herself.

"I think I have a plan," she said to Linda and Susan, "but all three of us have to cooperate or it won't work."

The next morning was Saturday. The breakfast table was crowded. Dolores, who had spent the night with Jill, was talking about the movie they were all going to see that afternoon. Ricky came to the table last. His hair was slicked back with water. *That's probably so Dolores will notice him,* thought Molly. But she didn't say anything to Ricky. She was still too mad about what he had done the night before.

Susan was the first to start the plan to get back at

Ricky. She asked Mrs. McIntire for three big brown bags. "We need them to hold our Halloween treats," she said with a look at Ricky. Mrs. McIntire gave her the bags.

Linda had a harder job to do. She had to keep Ricky out of his room for a while after breakfast. "Can I watch you shoot baskets?" she asked Ricky. "I want to learn how."

"Girls can't play basketball," answered Ricky rudely.

"Ricky!" said Mrs. McIntire. "What an unfriendly thing to say! You march outside like a gentleman and show Linda how to shoot baskets. She is our guest."

"Yes, ma'am," said Ricky.

He and Linda went outside. Mrs. McIntire walked with Brad to the mailbox around the corner to mail a letter to Dad. Dolores followed Jill up to her room to listen to records.

As soon as Jill's door closed, Molly and Susan dashed into Ricky's room. They flung open the top drawer of his dresser and dumped his underwear into a brown bag. They turned his laundry bag upside down on the floor, gathered the underwear and dirty socks from the pile, and stuffed them into the other two bags. They made one last quick check to be sure the room did not look disturbed before they rushed back to Molly's room.

The window in Molly's room looked out over the back door and driveway, where Ricky was shooting baskets and Linda was watching. Molly opened the window wide. "Okay, go on," she whispered to Susan.

"I can't do it," hissed Susan. "I'm too scared. And it's lying."

"Go *on*, Susan," said Molly. "You *have* to do it. Linda and I will never speak to you again if you don't. Just cross your fingers, then it's not a lie."

"Okay," said Susan. She went and knocked softly on Jill's door. Jill and Dolores were inside practicing the rhumba.

"What do *you* want!" Jill asked Susan.

"Well," said Susan, "I thought you'd like to know that Russ Campbell is at the corner in his car. He told me to run in here and tell you two—I mean *ask* you—if you wanted to go for a ride with him."

"Russ Campbell?" Jill and Dolores shrieked. Russ Campbell was the senior football star at Montgomery

High School, where Jill and Dolores were freshmen. A ride in Russ Campbell's car was a dream come true for them.

"Oh, how do I look?" asked Jill in a panic.

"You look fine," said Dolores. "Gosh, I'm glad we curled our hair last night!"

"Let's go!" said Jill. "Let's go before Russ changes his mind."

"Okay!" said Dolores. The girls galloped down the stairs, but just before they went out the back door they slowed down, patted their hair, smoothed their skirts, and straightened their shoulders.

Susan ran back to Molly's room. "Get ready! They're on their way outside!"

Seconds later, as Dolores and Jill came out the back door, Molly and Susan leaned way out the window, yelled as loud as they could, and turned the big brown bags upside down. Underwear and T-shirts filled the air like giant, floppy snowflakes. Dozens of socks tumbled down. A T-shirt got caught in the basketball hoop. A dirty sock landed on Jill's shoulder. Some plaid undershorts landed right on Dolores's head.

"What's *this*?" asked Dolores in disgust as she lifted

the underwear off her head with the very tips of her fingers.

Molly, Susan, and Linda chanted:

"I see London,
I see France,
Those are Ricky's underpants!"

"I'll get you!" Ricky yelled back. "You'll be sorry! This is war! This is really war! I'll—"

Suddenly Ricky stopped. He stood still in the driveway. Jill and Dolores stopped, too.

Molly and Susan leaned out of the window to see why. There was Mrs. McIntire, standing at the end of the driveway with Brad. Her face was as hard and cold and white as a marble statue. "Uh-oh," said Susan. She slid down to the floor next to Molly.

Mrs. McIntire looked up at the window. "Come down here at once, girls," she said sternly. "Jill and Dolores, I want you to hear this, too."

In seconds, everyone stood on the back steps. Molly's legs were shaky. No one said anything. Then Mrs. McIntire began to speak.

"Until there are no more tricks in this house, there will be no more treats," said Mrs. McIntire. "Instead of going to the movies, Ricky, you will spend your day raking the yard. Make sure you rake up the Halloween mess you made—all the bits of costumes, all the ruined food. Susan, Linda, and Molly, you will spend your day doing Ricky's laundry. I want everything washed, hung out to dry, folded, and put away by the end of the afternoon. Jill and Dolores, you will take care of Brad."

Mrs. McIntire paused. She looked straight at Molly, then straight at Ricky. "I suppose these tricks you have been playing on each other don't seem very serious to you. But they are mean, childish, and wasteful. I'm disappointed in you, but more than that, I'm sad and discouraged. If we can't get along together, who can?"

Molly looked at Ricky. Ricky looked at his mother. "This fighting has to stop," Mrs. McIntire went on. "This is exactly what starts wars—this meanness, anger, and revenge. Two sides decide to get even and end up hurting each other. There's enough war and fighting in the world, and I won't have any more of it in our house. Is that understood?"

Everyone mumbled, "Yes, ma'am."

"All right, then," said Mrs. McIntire. "Get to work." She went inside.

Molly stood up and faced Ricky. "Give me your un—uh, your things," she said.

"Here," said Ricky. "I think that's all of them." He pushed the bundle into her arms.

"Okay," said Molly. "Listen, we didn't—I mean, we didn't want to keep fighting with you, exactly. We were just mad. We wanted to embarrass you. We shouldn't have done it. I'm sorry. I really am."

"It's okay," said Ricky. "I guess I deserved it." He began to smile a little. "Your trick was mean, but you know, it was funny, too." He laughed. "I'm kind of glad not to be fighting against you any more. You three have pretty good ideas, even if you are a bunch of triple dips. I guess it's better to be on your side than to be your enemy."

Molly grinned. "Thanks, Ricky," she said. She and Linda and Susan went inside.

It wasn't so bad doing Ricky's laundry. Molly, Linda, and Susan pretended they were three Cinderellas before the ball. So, in a way, Molly got to be Cinderella for Halloween after all. And later, when the girls went outside to hang the laundry on the clothesline, Mrs. McIntire came out to help them.

"It sort of looks like an underwear tree, doesn't it?" she said when they were finished. She smiled down at Molly, who turned and gave her a hug. Her mother was right: It was much better not to be fighting.

Eight Times Seven

✪ CHAPTER 5 ✪

olly loved to look at her teacher, Miss Campbell. Miss Campbell's hair was brown and so smooth and shiny it reminded Molly of dark, polished wood. Most of the time Miss Campbell wore her hair pinned on top of her head in a soft roll. But sometimes, like today, she wore it down in a pageboy. Her long, glossy curls just brushed her shoulders and swung like a dancer's skirt when she turned her head quickly. Molly touched the ends of her own hair. *Sticks,* she thought. *My hair is as straight as sticks. When Molly* grew up, she wanted her hair to look just like Miss Campbell's, but it had a long way to go.

Today Miss Campbell was wearing a bright red sweater exactly the color of six red geraniums that stood saluting the sun on the windowsill. Miss Campbell sat up straight on the piano stool and sang along with the class in a clear, firm voice:

> *America, America!*
> *God shed His grace on thee.*
> *And crown thy good with brotherhood*
> *From sea to shining sea!*

Then she smiled at the class. "Excellent! Now let's get to work. We have a great deal to do today."

Molly watched Miss Campbell write "Things to Do Today" on the blackboard. When some teachers wrote that, it looked like a scold or the heading to a long list of tiresome tasks. But when Miss Campbell wrote it, in round, even letters, it looked like a challenge. Wake up! Sharpen your pencils! The day is beginning! Miss Campbell expected her third-graders to be on their toes. She often said, "School is your war duty. Being a good student is as important as being a good soldier."

Miss Campbell wrote:

Geography

Howie Munson began waving his hand wildly, as if

he were drowning at sea and Miss Campbell were the rescue ship.

"Yes, Howard?" Miss Campbell said.

Howie stood up next to his desk. "Miss Campbell, ma'am, don't forget, yesterday you said we could have a multiplication bee."

Molly groaned to herself. Howie said "multiplication bee" as if it would be a big treat, like cupcakes for lunch. Molly absolutely hated multiplication bees. They made her so nervous that she forgot problems she knew by heart, even the easy ones like two times two. She hid her hands in her lap and crossed her fingers. *Please let her say no,* she prayed.

But Miss Campbell was laughing. "You're right, Howard. We will have a multiplication contest today. I have a big gold badge for the student who wins the contest, too!"

"I bet it will be me, Miss Campbell," said Howie. "I know 'em all! Just ask me anything!"

"We'll see, Howard," said Miss Campbell. "But right now, please be seated."

Howie sat down at his desk. He was so excited that he raised his clenched fists above his head like a prize fighter. "Howard," said Miss Campbell firmly, "please save your celebration until after the contest."

Howie sat right behind Molly. There were twenty-one students in Molly's class, ten girls and eleven boys. They were seated in alphabetical order at desks arranged in four straight rows. Molly sat at the middle desk in the third row, in back of Grace Littlefield, the new girl who was as quiet as a mouse. Linda and Susan were also in Miss Campbell's class.

The classroom was large and square, smelling of chalk dust, books, and turtle food. It was painted pale green, with a high ceiling and a shiny wooden floor. Along one wall, above the bookshelves, there were windows. They were tall windows, twice as tall as Molly. It was quite a job to open them at the top. You had to pull them down with a long pole that had a metal knob at the end. It was tricky to fit the knob into the hole all the way at the top of the window, and you had to be strong because the pole was heavy. Then you had to pull on it with all your weight to make the window open even a crack. Being asked to open the top windows was an honor that Miss Campbell gave to everyone in turn. It didn't matter how big you were, or how well you had managed the job in the past. Everyone got a chance, fair and square. Her fairness was one of the things everyone liked most about Miss Campbell.

Miss Campbell's desk was in the front of the room, right under the flag. But she hardly ever sat at it. She walked around the room as she talked, or stood by the bookshelves, the blackboard, the piano, or a student's desk. Molly loved it when Miss Campbell stopped at her desk. She smelled like peppermints. Up close, her hands were smooth, square, and small. They were very neat and tidy, just like Miss Campbell. When Miss Campbell explained things—like nouns and verbs, and when *i* comes before *e*—she made them seem neat and tidy, too. With Miss Campbell leading the way, the school day marched along smoothly from the first song in the morning to the last dismissal bell.

Right now, Miss Campbell was standing in the front of the room by the maps. The maps were rolled up on poles like window shades. Molly loved it when Miss Campbell pulled down one of the maps. The sun would catch a ring on her finger and send rainbows of light dancing on the walls. Susan, Linda, and Molly spent a lot of time discussing that ring. Susan thought it was an engagement ring and that Miss Campbell was engaged to marry a soldier who was off fighting the war. Linda said nobody knew for sure if that was true or not. Molly hoped very much that it was. She hoped that Miss Campbell's soldier would come home soon and that her teacher would ask Molly to be the flower girl in her wedding. Molly would carry a little basket of flower petals, or maybe she'd hold the train of Miss Campbell's wedding dress. Any day now, Miss Campbell would come to her and ask, "Molly? . . ."

"Molly?"

Molly sat up straight at her desk. Miss Campbell *was* asking her something, but it wasn't about flower petals. "Molly, your mind is a million miles away. Perhaps while you're bringing it back to our classroom, someone else can tell us the name of the capital city of England. Grace, can you help us?"

"London!" squeaked Grace, proud to know the answer.

Hmph! thought Molly. *Everybody knows that.*

"That's right, Grace," Miss Campbell said. On the map, she pointed to London with a long, rubber-tipped pointer. "And who can tell me why it's important for us to know about England and London?"

Molly shot her hand up before anyone else.

"Molly?"

Molly stood next to her desk to answer. "Because of the war. America and England are fighting together in the war against Germany. We're helping England. I know because my father's there working in a hospital. The Germans are bombing England, and my father is taking care of the soldiers who get hurt in battles."

Molly stopped talking and sat down. She didn't really like to talk about her father being in England. It made her remember that he was in danger and very, very far away. Sometimes she worried that he might get hurt by a German bomb. She looked at the map. The ocean between America and England looked awfully big. And England looked awfully small, and not very safe. It was so little, in such a big ocean, so near Germany and so far from home.

Miss Campbell smiled at Molly. "Very good, Molly. Thank you for telling the class about your father. You must be very proud of him." She turned to the blackboard. "Molly's right. The United States and England are *allies.* That means we're working together to beat Germany." Miss Campbell wrote on the board:

Allies—People who work together
for the same goal

"America is cooperating with England because we hope we can get the job of winning the war done faster if we help each other," Miss Campbell said. "Now, for next Tuesday, I'd like you to write three paragraphs about cooperation and why it's a good idea for people to work together. Tell how allies can help each other. Remember to indent at the beginning of every new paragraph."

Woody Halsey raised his hand. "Does spelling count?" he asked.

"Yes, Woody, spelling counts," said Miss Campbell. "Use the dictionary. Be as careful as you can be. And speaking of 'be's,' it's time for the multiplication bee! Line up quietly."

Howie Munson was the first one out of his seat. "Boys against girls!" he blurted out.

"Let's calm down, please, Howard. Boys, line up by

the windows. Girls, line up by the door. Woody, there will be no pushing in line, please."

Everyone chattered happily as the teams rushed to line up. Molly walked over to the girls' line and stood on the very end. *Maybe I could step back into the cloakroom and hide,* she thought. *Maybe no one would miss me.*

"Nine times six!" Miss Campbell said, and the race was on.

Molly's stomach felt as if it were full of sloshing water. *Maybe I'll throw up,* she thought.

"Seven times seven!"

"Forty-nine!"

"Four times eight!"

"Thirty-two!"

Hardly anyone waited even a second. Molly wondered how people could slap those answers down so quickly. She leaned against the bulletin board that had a display of the planets on it. *I wish I were on another planet right now,* she thought. *I bet no one on Mars cares about multiplication.*

The girl behind Molly gave her a little shove. "Move up," she said. "You're right after Susan."

Molly gulped. Susan was next.

"Fifty-four," said Susan smoothly. All the girls clapped and patted her on the back as she walked to the end of the line.

"Nine times twelve!"

Woody Halsey squinted at the ceiling. "One . . . hundred . . . and . . . eight," he said.

"Okay!" said the other boys. "Good going, Woody!"

Now it was Molly's turn.

"Eight times seven!"

Molly froze. The eights! Her worst! She hated the eights!

"Eight times seven," Miss Campbell repeated.

Molly closed her eyes. *Eight times seven. Eight times seven. Probably in the fifties somewhere,* she thought.

"Uh . . . fifty . . . nine?" Molly offered timidly. She thought she was probably wrong. Sure enough, all the girls groaned. Howie jumped out of line and yelled, "Fifty-six! Fifty-six! Eight times seven is fifty-six!"

"Why, Molly," said Miss Campbell. "I think you need a little more practice with the multiplication flash cards. You'd better review your eights until you know them."

Molly didn't say anything. She walked to her desk and sat down, stiff with shame. The multiplication contest went on around her. Questions and answers buzzed back and forth across the room like bees to a hive. Molly wanted to put her fingers in her ears to block out the numbers. "Nine times nine!" "Thirteen times three!" Nobody else missed a problem for a long time. Then slowly, one by one, others took their seats. Finally, only Howie and Alison were left.

"All right," said Miss Campbell. "One more problem, and whoever answers first is the winner. Ready?"

Alison and Howie nodded.

"Twelve times thirteen."

Howie bit his lip and scowled.

"One hundred fifty-six," said Alison calmly.

"Hurray! We win!" cried all the girls except Molly. They all ran up to Alison to hug her. Everyone except Molly, even the boys, clapped when Miss Campbell pinned a big, shiny gold badge on Alison's sweater. "Excellent work, Alison. I'm proud of you."

Alison beamed. Molly saw her look down at the gold badge and touch it with her fingers. Molly looked away. She pulled her three-ring notebook out of her desk and opened it to a blank piece of paper. In big numbers she wrote:

$$\begin{array}{r} 8 \\ \times\,7 \\ \hline 56 \end{array}$$

Lend a Hand

he day dragged on forever after the multiplication bee. At lunch, Molly felt as if she had a sore throat. She opened her lunch bag and looked inside. Mrs. Gilford had packed a peanut butter and jelly sandwich. Molly took a bite. It got stuck in her throat. She decided she was probably getting the mumps.

In reading, which was usually Molly's favorite subject, she didn't get a chance to read out loud because Miss Campbell stopped the reading group early. Miss Campbell stood in the front of the room and raised both hands, the signal for quiet. All the rustling and chair squeaks and whispers stopped when she said, "Class, I have a special announcement to make, if I may have your attention, please."

Molly looked up. A special announcement? It was

something good, she could tell, because Miss Campbell's face looked pink and pleased.

"Our class has been invited to participate in a school-wide contest. It's called the Lend-a-Hand Contest. Every student is challenged to lend a hand to help the war effort. Every class will be divided into teams. You may divide yourself into teams in any way you wish."

"Boys against girls!" said Howie definitely. "Boys against girls!" All the boys murmured in agreement.

Miss Campbell waited for quiet. "Well, that will be fine if that's the way you want to do it. You may choose any kind of project you wish, but it must be something to help our soldiers in the war effort. At the end of the contest, the winning team will receive an award at a school assembly. Now, you have only one weekend to do the project from start to finish. Plan your projects today. Work on them tomorrow. Bring them in on Monday. Remember, you will be competing against boys and girls in the fourth and fifth grades, so be sure you choose a very good project to do, and work hard on it."

The classroom was awash in a sea of voices as the

teams discussed different ideas for their projects. Linda waved to Susan while Alison whispered to Grace. Woody sat on top of his desk, talking to Howie over Grace's head. Then Susan leaned over to Molly. "What should we do?" she asked.

"I don't know," said Molly. She tried to think of a spectacular project. Collect a thousand dollars and buy a War Bond? No, too hard. Roll bandages? Too boring. Collect newspapers? Everyone did that. Oh, the third-grade girls *had* to win the contest. Just think how pleased Miss Campbell would be! Molly would work harder than anyone else on the project, and then when they won, she'd have her picture in the newspaper, probably with Miss Campbell. THIRD-GRADE GIRL LENDS A BIG HAND TO WAR EFFORT, it would say under the picture. And Miss Campbell would send the picture to the soldier she was engaged to, and he would write back, "Let's ask Molly McIntire to be in our wedding . . ."

"What a wonderful idea, Alison!" Miss Campbell was saying. "I think that's a fine project. You certainly have *your* thinking cap on today."

On the blackboard, Miss Campbell wrote:

❂ A Winning Spirit ❂

Girls—Knit socks

Knit socks! Molly thought. *That's a terrible idea!* Molly knew all about knitting socks. Well, she didn't really know *all* about it, but she knew it was hard. Molly had struggled through knitting lessons with Mrs. Gilford. She had not been able to finish even one sock. Socks took a long time. They were complicated. By the time Mrs. Gilford finished a sock, it looked as if it had already marched a million miles. The third-grade girls would never win the contest if they chose knitting socks as a project.

Molly had to say something. But as she started to raise her hand, Susan leaned over and whispered, "Won't that be fun? We can make hundreds of socks if we all knit this weekend."

Molly brought her hand down. No one would listen to her now. All the other girls were gathered in a bunch around Alison's desk. They decided to unravel old sweaters or ask their mothers for yarn scraps they could use. Alison was smiling and nodding, writing something on a piece of paper.

✪ Lend a Hand ✪

That Alison! thought Molly. *It would be her idea. Always trying to get in good with Miss Campbell!*

Well, Molly wasn't going to let Alison tell her what to do. She wasn't going to let Alison lead all the girls in the class into some dumb project that wouldn't even work. Molly sat at her desk thinking hard. It wasn't easy to concentrate because all around her the boys were talking loudly about their project. Woody Halsey wanted to dig an air-raid shelter for the school. "All's we'd need would be some shovels," he kept saying.

Howie's idea finally won out. He suggested the boys collect tinfoil and send it to be made into tanks and trucks for the soldiers. "We'll make a ball of tinfoil six feet wide," he said grandly. "We'll roll it up the aisle during the assembly." The boys were impressed. On the blackboard, Miss Campbell wrote:

Boys—Collect tinfoil for ball

When the dismissal bell rang, Miss Campbell said, "Thank you for working hard today. Good luck on your projects! Now line up quietly! I'll see you Monday."

Molly led the line of third-graders marching down

the stairs and out of the school building into the pale November sunshine. *Knit socks!* she thought. *It's a bad idea, it really is.* Molly didn't think that just because it was Alison's idea, either. She hopped on one foot and then the other, waiting for Linda and Susan. *I won't knit socks,* Molly decided. *I'll think up another project that will win the contest. Then Alison and Miss Campbell will see who has her thinking cap on.*

Molly, Linda, and Susan usually walked home together. On most days, they stopped and played at Molly's house because Mrs. Gilford was there to keep an eye on them. Mrs. McIntire usually did not get home from her job at the Red Cross until dinnertime, and both Linda's mother and Susan's mother worked in an airplane factory every afternoon.

When the girls got to the back door of Molly's house, Molly flung it open, took a deep breath, and shouted, "Hurray! Bread day!"

Mrs. Gilford replied with three brisk commands: "Come in. Wipe your feet. Sit at the table like ladies."

The kitchen was steamy. It smelled like warm raisins. Mrs. Gilford stood at the table behind an army of bowls and measuring cups. She nodded to the girls and pointed with the end of her wooden spoon to the three plates on the table in front of them. "There are your sample slices," she said.

On each plate was a thick, round, brown piece of bread, heavy with fat raisins. "It's round!" said Susan.

"Boston Brown Bread!" replied Mrs. Gilford. "Baked in an old coffee tin. And not a speck of sugar or butter in it!"

Molly picked up her piece of bread and took a bite. "Mmmmm! This is a good one, Mrs. Gilford."

"I like this bread, too," said Linda.

"Me, too," said Susan. "It tastes like Christmas."

"I like the smell," said Molly with her mouth full. "If I had perfume, I'd want it to smell just exactly like this."

"Hmph! You'd probably have all the dogs in the neighborhood following you around," snorted Mrs. Gilford. But Molly could tell she was pleased.

Making bread was one of the things Mrs. Gilford did to help the war effort. Every week she tried a new bread recipe. Molly, Linda, and Susan were her official testing committee. Out of all the breads Mrs. Gilford had tried so far, only one had not met with everyone's approval. That was "Red Bread" made with tomato juice. Molly and Linda begged Mrs. Gilford never to make it again. Susan voted for it because it was pink.

Making bread from scratch during wartime was not easy. Mrs. Gilford had to figure out substitutes for some ingredients that were hard to get, like butter and sugar. But Mrs. Gilford rose to the challenge just as her loaves of bread rose high and brown and delicious. Of all the changes the war had brought to the McIntire household, the only one Molly could absolutely positively say she liked was Mrs. Gilford's homemade bread.

Today Mrs. Gilford had a pamphlet called *How to Bake by the Ration Book* propped up between a milk bottle and a sack of flour. Molly watched Mrs. Gilford sifting some flour through a strainer. She was making a small snowstorm fall right into a bowl on the kitchen table. It looked like fun—you could make a mess, but it wouldn't get you into trouble.

"Can I sift it?" she asked Mrs. Gilford.

"*May* I sift it, and no, you may not. Not in your school clothes. You'd be covered all over with flour. Trot upstairs, put on your play clothes, and *then* you may sign up to be a doughboy."

"That would take too much time," said Linda.

"I don't think I'd better," said Molly. "We have to work on our project."

Mrs. Gilford looked up. "What project?"

"Well, there's a Lend-a-Hand Contest at school. We're supposed to do a project to help the war effort. We only have this weekend to do it. Whoever does the best project wins a prize," explained Molly.

"And what's your project?" asked Mrs. Gilford with interest.

"We don't know yet," said Molly.

"Yes we do," said Susan. She gave Molly a puzzled look. "We're knitting socks, hundreds and hundreds of socks. Just like you do, Mrs. Gilford."

Mrs. Gilford poured milk into a measuring cup. "I see," she said. "Well, good luck to you. You may take another slice of bread if you wish. No crumbs on the floor, please. Come to me if you decide you need knitting needles and yarn."

"Thank you, Mrs. Gilford," the girls said. They each took another slice of bread. Then they went outside and walked over to the garage. There was a storage room above the garage, and the girls liked to talk there. It was a private place they used as a clubhouse. They climbed the stairs to the storage room, already nibbling their second slices of bread.

Top Secret

he garage was cold, especially compared to the warm kitchen. It was dark, too, because the only light came from the door at one end of the storage room and a window at the other end. The girls couldn't stand up straight except in the very middle of the room because the ceiling was sloped like the sides of a tent.

The storage room smelled of dust, mothballs, and dried-up paper. It was filled with things waiting to be fixed up, thrown out, or needed again. There was a big trunk with one latch broken, boxes full of books, games with pieces missing, and a tarnished tennis trophy. There was a chest of drawers with a mirror on top that made you look green and speckled, a box labeled "Curtains—Too Short," and a rolltop desk with no drawers. Everything looked ghostly because everything was covered with a gray blanket of dust.

The girls had pushed two old love seats together, face-to-face, under the window. The love seats were not very comfortable because the springs and padding had fallen out of the bottom of them. But they had high, curved backs, so when they were pushed together they made a sort of boat that floated in a dusty sea.

Linda climbed aboard first. "Knitting!" she groaned. "I'm going to be terrible at this project. I *hate* knitting. Everything I ever knitted came out looking like a piece of chewed string."

"Oh, I think knitting is fun," said Susan. "And socks are cute."

"Have you ever knitted a sock?" asked Molly.

"Well, no," said Susan. "But I've seen people do it."

"Yeah, well it's *hard*," said Molly. "I've watched Mrs. Gilford do it. You have to use three needles sometimes, and count stitches, and purl, and turn the heel, and lots of other complicated things."

Susan looked at Molly for a while. "I'll bet you don't like it just because it's Alison's idea," she said. "You're jealous because Alison won the multiplication bee and Miss Campbell gave her the gold badge today, and you did the worst of anybody."

"That's not true!" said Molly.

"It is too!" said Susan.

"It is not!"

"It is too!"

"Cut it out," said Linda. "It doesn't matter whose idea it is. I still can't knit."

"I think we should do another project," said Molly.

"We can't," said Susan. "All the girls are doing socks. It's our Lend-a-Hand project. Miss Campbell would be mad at us. *Everyone* would be mad at us if we didn't do socks."

"Listen," said Molly. "Those girls are crazy if they think they can each knit even one pair of socks by Monday. They can't possibly do it. The whole third grade will look terrible. They'll be grateful to us if we do another project. Miss Campbell will be proud of us."

Susan was doubtful. "Well, I don't know."

"Look, you want to win the contest, don't you?"

"Yes, but—"

"Well, believe me, there's no way the third-grade girls can ever win by knitting socks. It's up to us. We have to do another project and win the contest for the third-grade girls." Molly was firm.

"You make it sound so easy to win," said Linda. "What other project can we do that would be so great? Build a fighter plane or something?"

Susan giggled. "We could become spies and go on a mission and steal top secret information from the enemy."

"Hey!" said Molly. "That's it! We sort of *could* be secret agents."

"What do you mean?" asked Susan.

"Well," said Molly, "we're secret agents because nobody knows what we're doing, right? Just us three. And our mission is our project. Only instead of stealing information, we can collect something, something like—"

"Tops! Bottletops!" interrupted Linda. "Get it? *Top* Secret. We'll be Top Secret Agents."

"Yes!" said Molly. "That's it! We'll collect bottletops for scrap metal. They use scrap metal to make tanks and battleships and things, so it's good for the war effort. We'll collect at least a hundred bottletops, and we'll surprise everybody in school on Monday.

And we'll win the contest, and Miss Campbell will be pleased with us."

"Top Secret Agents!" said Susan. "Just like in the movies. We can wear matching clothes. You know, spy clothes—dark pants and dark shirts—and send notes in a secret code, and have a secret hideout."

"Right here!" said Molly. "This can be our hideout."

"We should have a secret handshake, too," said Linda. "And we can never show anybody what it is."

"And we can't tell anybody what our secret project is," said Molly. "We have to be sworn to secrecy."

"Okay, let's swear," said Linda. "Come on! A solemn oath!" She raised her right hand. Molly and Susan did, too. "I promise never to tell anyone—"

"Shhh!" Molly interrupted. "I hear something!"

"What is it?" asked Susan. "An enemy spy!"

Molly waved to her to be quiet. She crept over to the window. "It's Alison! Alison Hargate is knocking on the kitchen door!"

"I want to see," said Linda, moving to the window.

"Get down!" Molly commanded. She and Linda knelt by the window.

"Hey, look!" said Linda. "Alison has a big white envelope in her hand."

They looked down at Alison from their hideout. They saw Mrs. Gilford come to the door, wiping her hands on her apron. Alison showed Mrs. Gilford the envelope. Mrs. Gilford nodded and squinted up at the garage, then pointed right at the window. The girls ducked. They heard footsteps coming toward the garage.

"She's coming this way!" whispered Linda.

"Quick! Hide!" Molly hissed.

"But—" said Susan.

"Hurry *up*," ordered Molly. "If she sees us, it will ruin everything!" She slithered under one of the love seats. Linda hid behind a trunk. Susan knelt in a corner, then popped up like a jack-in-the-box and ran over to hide under the rolltop desk.

Molly's heart was pounding. It smelled musty under the couch, and the broken springs dug into her back. She heard the door open, but all she could see were Alison's feet. The feet came into the room and stopped.

"Molly?"

Molly held her breath.

The feet hesitated, then turned and went out the door. Molly could hear them hurrying down the stairs. All her breath came out in one big sigh.

"The coast is clear," she said. Then she wiggled out from under the love seat like a snake going backward. Linda went back to the window and reported on Alison's movements.

"She's knocking on the door again. Wait! No, she isn't. She's not knocking. She's just . . . she's just leaving the envelope stuck on the doorknob. I guess she's scared to talk to Mrs. Gilford again. Now she's running away, down the driveway." Linda turned away from the window. "She's gone."

"Well, I don't see why we had to hide," huffed Susan. She had dust in her hair and dirt streaked across the back of her coat. "It's only Alison."

"Alison's not a Top Secret Agent," Molly explained. "If she saw us up here, she'd ask what we're doing, and pretty soon our whole secret project wouldn't be secret anymore. It wouldn't be a surprise. It wouldn't be anything at all, and we'd be just like everyone else. Remember, we promised to keep it secret."

A Winning Spirit ✪

"Come on," said Linda. "Let's go! I can't wait to see what's in that envelope." She was already halfway out the door. Molly and Susan followed close behind into the chill November twilight.

Mrs. Gilford had already turned on the light next to the kitchen door. The girls huddled under it as Molly opened the envelope and pulled out a card. "It's an invitation," she said.

"Oooooooh! Let me see," said Susan. She stood on tiptoe and leaned over Molly's shoulder.

You are invited to
A Knitting Bee
To work on your socks
for the Lend-a-Hand Contest from
nine o'clock to three o'clock tomorrow at
Alison's house. Lunch and other refreshments too!
(Bring your own yarn and needles.)

Molly's hands were stiff and cold. Susan took the invitation from her and held it under the light. "Gee, I bet that will be fun," she said. "A knitting bee at Alison's house."

"Probably great refreshments, too," said Linda.

"Oh, I don't know," said Molly. "I don't think it will be great. All they'll do is sit and knit, knit and sit all day. I think we'll have more fun collecting bottle-tops."

"Well, I want to go home and see if I got an invitation, too," said Susan.

"I'm cold," said Linda. "I'm going home, too."

"Okay," said Molly. "Meet back here at nine o'clock sharp tomorrow."

Linda and Susan waved good-bye and hurried off into the gray evening. Molly looked at the invitation one more time, then crumpled it up, put it in her coat pocket, and went inside.

Spies and Allies

lip, plop, plip, plop, plip . . . Molly rolled over in bed and opened her eyes to a weepy, wet day. The windows of her room were blurred like teary eyes. *Oh, no,* she thought. *What a day to be outside, going door to door collecting bottletops!*

Molly got up and put on her spy outfit—dark blue corduroy pants and a dark plaid shirt—and thumped down the stairs to the kitchen.

On cold, rainy Saturdays, Molly's mother always made a warm breakfast. She believed children needed food that would stick to their ribs. Today she made thick, hot oatmeal.

"Why are you wearing that good plaid shirt to-day?" Mrs. McIntire asked Molly. "Mrs. Gilford just ironed it. Why don't you save it for school?"

"I need to wear it today, Mom," said Molly. "I'll be

careful. We're working on our project."

"What project is that?" Mrs. McIntire asked. She put a bowl of oatmeal in front of Molly and another in front of Ricky. Ricky began pouring honey on top of his oatmeal with one hand and filling a glass of tomato juice with the other.

"It's for school," said Molly. "Linda and Susan and I are doing a Lend-a-Hand project. Everyone is doing something for the war effort this weekend. There's a contest to see who has the best project."

"That sounds very worthwhile," said Mrs. McIntire.

"Sounds like a dumb elementary school contest to me," said Ricky. He was in the seventh grade. "What are you triple dips going to do, sign up to be monkeys in the zoo?" Ricky pretended his spoon was a banana and began to peel it. "Ooooh, ooh, oooh," he said as he scratched the top of his head like a chimpanzee.

"That's enough, Ricky," said Mrs. McIntire.

"Very funny," said Molly. "*That* wouldn't help win the war. For your information, we have a very good project."

"Yeah? What is it?" Ricky asked.

"I can't tell."

"I can't tell," mimicked Ricky in a high voice. "Well, just don't touch any of *my* stuff." Ricky pointed to himself with the hand that was holding the glass of tomato juice. Some of the juice sloshed over the edge of the glass onto his shirt. Ricky clutched at the red stain. "Oooh, ya got me!" he said. He jerked his head back, closed his eyes, and slumped off the edge of his chair onto the floor. "Dead," he said.

Molly giggled.

"Off with that shirt, young man," Mrs. McIntire said calmly. "That juice will stain if I don't get rid of it right away."

As Ricky took off his shirt, Molly rinsed her oatmeal bowl at the sink, dried her hands, and went to the closet to get her school bag, raincoat, and hat.

"Boots, too," said Mrs. McIntire without looking up from the sink.

Molly groaned. She didn't think real spies had to wear boots. But she took hers out of the closet and sat on the kitchen floor to put them on.

Molly had not used her boots since last winter, and they were a little dusty. The toe of her saddle shoe went in, but no matter how she yanked and pulled and pushed, her whole shoe would not fit inside her boot. She got up and hip-hopped over to her mother. "Look, Mom," she said. "My boots won't go on over my new saddle shoes. I guess I can't wear boots today."

Mrs. McIntire knelt down and tried to wiggle the boot on to Molly's foot. It would not budge. "Well," she said as she stood up. "You can't wear *these.* They're too small for you now."

"I'll have to get new ones," said Molly. "Maybe I can get red boots this year."

Mrs. McIntire stood up. She fastened the top button on Molly's raincoat. "I'm afraid not, dear," she said. "There are no rubber boots in the stores. I've looked. They're not being made."

"But why?" asked Molly.

"Because of the war," her mother said. "The rubber is needed to make things for the fighting men. Things like life rafts for battleships and life jackets for sailors. There just isn't enough rubber left over to make red rubber boots for nine-year-old girls." Mrs. McIntire leaned into the closet. "You'll have to wear Ricky's boots today." She held up Ricky's old black boots.

"My boots?" said Ricky.

"But, Mom," said Molly. "Those are boys' boots. They're ugly. They're—"

"Molly," Mrs. McIntire interrupted. "Think of it as a sacrifice you're making for the war effort." She handed the boots to Molly.

Molly sighed. She took the boots.

"And don't wreck them," said Ricky. "Or get perfume on them or anything."

Molly and her mother had to laugh. "Don't worry. I won't," Molly said. She pulled on Ricky's boots. They were clumsy, heavy boots with rusted buckles. The buckles fastened up the front, not on the side like girls' boots. They were a little bit too big, so Molly clomped like a horse as she made her way to the door.

"Good-bye, Mom," she said. "I probably won't be home for lunch. We'll be too busy to stop."

"All right," said Mrs. McIntire. "Be careful. Don't go into a stranger's house. Be home by three o'clock."

"Okay," said Molly. She went outside. Linda and Susan were coming up the driveway. Susan waddled like a plump duck under her big red umbrella. "My mother made me wear two sweaters under my raincoat," she complained. "I can hardly move."

"*My* mother wouldn't let me wear my dark shirt," said Linda. "She didn't have time to wash it. She's been working the late shift at the factory."

"And I have to wear these horrible boots of Ricky's," said Molly. "Oh, well, let's get started." She held up her school bag. "I hope this is big enough to hold all the bottletops," she said.

"Can't we take a break?" asked Susan. "I'm so hot."

"I'm so *cold*," said Linda.

"We can't take a break because we haven't started yet," said Molly. "Come on. Real secret agents have to work in the rain all the time."

There were seven houses on Molly's block. The girls trudged up to each one, rang the doorbell, and asked for bottletops.

At the first house, Mrs. Silvano said she didn't have any bottletops, but did they want old newspapers? They said no, thank you very much.

Billy Ruckstein answered the door at the next house. He was only four. He said yes, they did have bottletops. Then he ran off and came back with a top still connected to a whole bottle of ginger ale. The girls told him the top had to be off the bottle already, but thanked him very much anyway.

They walked on to the next house. Mr. Koloski said he had two bottletops, but he needed them himself. He was a Boy Scout troop leader, and the Boy Scouts were collecting bottletops for scrap metal, too.

Finally, Mrs. Keller gave them six bottletops she had been saving but had never gotten around to turning in. And Mrs. Leaming gave them four. She said if they wanted more they should come back next Saturday, because she was having a party then and she'd have lots of bottletops after the party.

By the time they'd gone to all seven houses on the block they had cold hands, wet legs, tired feet, and ten bottletops in Molly's school bag.

"Let's count them," said Susan. She handed her umbrella to Linda.

"What for?" said Linda. "We know perfectly well there are only ten."

"I know, but I want to see them," said Susan. She dug her hands into the school bag and pulled out two handfuls. Molly and Linda watched as she dropped the bottletops into the bag one by one. "One, two, three, four, five, six, seven, eight, nine, ten," she said as they clinked against one another. "I didn't think it would be so hard to get a hundred."

"We'll just have to keep trying," said Molly. "We can't give up now. Let's go to the next block."

Bottletops were scarce on the next block, too. No one was home at two houses. At one house, a man came to the door in a painter's hat. He was spattered all over with blue paint. He said if he *did* have any bottletops he'd never be able to find them because the whole house was torn up and in a mess. The girls peeked past him to see if that was true. It was.

One nice lady holding a baby gave them two apple juice bottletops and let them shake hands with the baby. A smiling old lady said they were sweet girls and gave them each one bottletop. As they left, Molly noticed two blue stars hung in her window. "She has *two* people from her family fighting in the war," Molly said.

"We have one blue star for my father," said Linda. "The people next door have a gold star because their son got killed." Molly looked back at the old lady's house. It seemed to be waiting for happy, noisy young people to come back and fill it with fun again.

At the next house, a teenage boy holding half a chicken sandwich pulled a bottletop out of his pocket, handed it to Molly, and closed the door without saying a word. "Did you see that sandwich?" asked Linda as they headed down the walk. "I'm hungry. It's lunchtime. We have to stop now."

"Not yet," said Molly. "We only have sixteen bottletops."

"I'm tired," said Susan. "I can't go on any longer."

"Some secret agents *you* two make," said Molly. Her nose was runny. Ricky's boots were heavy. "Come on. Just one more block, and then we'll take a break for lunch."

Susan sighed. Linda shivered. Molly led the way across the street to the next block.

"Hey, you know who lives on this block?" Linda asked. "Alison Hargate."

"I know," said Molly. "We just won't go to her house to ask for bottletops."

"I bet Alison has lots of bottletops," said Susan. The girls were now standing right in front of Alison's house.

"I know what! Let's go peek in the window at the

knitting bee," said Linda. "It'll be fun! Just like real secret agents!"

"Yes!" said Susan. "Let's spy on them."

Molly hesitated. "What if someone sees us?" she asked. But Linda was already bent over, creeping behind a tall bush and heading toward a big window. Susan put her umbrella in the bush and followed Linda. Molly felt out of place standing on the sidewalk all alone, so she finally went, too.

When Molly bent over to sneak behind the bushes, the rain dripped down the back of her neck. It gave her goose bumps. Linda and Susan were on tiptoe, holding on to the window ledge, peering inside. Molly looked, too.

Oh, it was so warm and cozy in there! They were looking into Alison's living room, where a cheery fire blazed in the fireplace. All the other girls in their class were sitting cross-legged in a circle on the rug. They had bright balls of yarn in their laps and long slender knitting needles in their hands. The Hargates' maid knelt behind Grace Littlefield, her big capable hands guiding Grace's on the needles. Alison was laughing, and all the other girls looked happy.

"Look at that tray of sandwiches!" said Linda. "And cocoa and cookies, too!"

"It looks like fun," said Susan wistfully. "The yarn is pretty."

"I don't see any socks," said Molly.

"Look, Grace can't even hold her needles right," giggled Linda.

"WELL! What have we here?" boomed a voice very close by. The girls jumped.

It was Mrs. Hargate, Alison's mother! She was standing right behind them, blocking their path back to the sidewalk, holding a big black umbrella. Drips from the umbrella hit Molly right on the cheek. Mrs. Hargate had on very red lipstick.

"You girls are late for the knitting bee," said Mrs. Hargate. "But that doesn't matter. Come along! Alison was *so* worried when you didn't get here at nine with all the other gals. She was afraid you weren't coming *at all.* But I told her that you'd *never* be so rude. You'd never miss out on all the fun and not help on the project. I said I was sure you'd turn up, and I was right. Here you are!" Mrs. Hargate kept talking as she herded them inside like captured criminals. Linda, Molly, and

Susan didn't have time to say anything. Molly didn't know what to say anyway.

Before they knew it, the three girls were standing in the Hargates' front hall, the water dripping off their coats and forming small puddles around them. "Look who *I* found," Mrs. Hargate called to Alison in a very loud voice as she took off her coat. "Darling Linda, Susan, and Molly were waiting outside! Take off those sopping coats, girls. And the boots, too. Why, Molly, aren't those boots a teensy bit too big for you? Scoot along now. Go on in and join the party. I'll be in the den if you need me."

Molly, Linda, and Susan bumped into one another, each trying to be the last one to enter the living room. Alison jumped up from the circle and said, "Hi."

"Hi," mumbled Linda, Susan, and Molly.

"We were afraid you weren't coming," Alison said. "Where are your knitting needles and yarn?" She looked behind them, as if they might be hiding yarn and needles there as a surprise.

"We don't have any," said Linda.

"Oh, well, it doesn't matter," said Alison. "I have lots of extra needles, and none of us has used very much yarn yet. Sit down, and I'll get everything for you."

Molly, Linda, and Susan sat awkwardly on the edge of the couch behind the circle of knitters. They looked like three crows on a branch. "Here," Alison said as she handed them needles and yarn. "I hope the colors are okay. And I hope you're good knitters. We sure need some. How come you were so late?"

Linda looked at Molly. Molly looked at Susan. Susan twisted a strand of yarn around her finger. "Well," she said, "we're not doing knitting. I mean, we have another project. We're—"

Molly jabbed Susan with her elbow and Susan stopped talking.

Alison looked puzzled. "You're not making socks? You have *another* Lend-a-Hand project?"

Molly took a deep breath. "We're sort of just visiting you. We're doing a different project."

"What is it?" asked Alison.

"It's a secret," said Molly.

"Oh." Alison went back to knitting. Molly, Linda, and Susan just watched. The other girls knitted silently.

Molly noticed that none of the knitters had gotten

very far. Most of the girls had knitted only the top part of one sock. They were just getting to the hard part, the heel, where they needed to use three needles. What they had knitted didn't look at all like socks. They had knitted squares about the size of a doll's blanket.

A blanket! Molly sat up on the edge of the couch. That's what they should knit, not socks! They could knit squares, then sew them together to make a big blanket. They practically had enough squares already. A blanket was such a good idea! So much easier than socks! So much faster! But Molly didn't dare say anything. After all, it wasn't *her* project.

Suddenly, Grace Littlefield threw down her needles. She looked ready to cry. Everyone stared at her. "I can't do this," she wailed. "I just can't! It was hard enough with the two needles, but three is impossible! Every stitch I knit comes undone. I'll never make a whole sock, never!"

Molly felt sorry for Grace. She slid off the couch and sat on the floor next to her. "Socks are hard, Grace," she said. "But you know, you have a nice square here. If we—I mean, if *you*—all put your squares together, you could make a really nice blanket.

I saw Mrs. Gilford do it once. See, you just lay out the squares . . ."

"We're making *socks*," said Alison.

Molly sat back up on the couch.

"Wait," said one of the other girls. "Maybe Molly has a good idea. We all have squares already. If we each make just one or two more, we could make a big blanket."

"But how do we sew the squares together?" asked Alison.

"Oh, I know how to do *that*," said Linda. "You don't have to be able to knit to do *that*. You just need a big sewing needle."

"Oh, let's try it," said Grace. "A blanket is a good idea."

Molly jumped up. "We should have an assembly line," she said. "The best knitters keep knitting. Grace, you collect the squares and flatten them out. Linda, you and I will sew the squares together."

"I'll finish your square, Grace," said Susan.

"I'll go find a big sewing needle," said Alison.

All of a sudden, everyone was talking at once. The knitters clicked away on their needles, finishing square after square. Grace hurried from knitter to knitter, collecting, flattening, and organizing the finished squares. Molly and Linda sat on the couch. Linda sewed the brightly colored squares together into long strips. Molly sewed the strips together. Slowly, the knitted blanket grew until Molly had to drape it over the back of the couch. Finally, the needles were still.

All of the girls stood up and lifted the blanket to fold it. Susan held one edge up to her cheek. "I think this is the most beautiful blanket anyone ever made in the whole world."

"And we all did it. I don't even remember which squares I made now that they're all together," said Alison.

"But do you think a blanket can win the Lend-a-Hand Contest?" asked Mary Lou Dobbs. "Is a blanket a good war effort?"

"Oh, *yes*," said Molly. Her fingers were sore where she had pricked them with the needle, and her legs were stiff from sitting still so long. "Just this week we got a letter from my dad saying that they really need blankets in the hospitals. It gets pretty cold in England, and winter is coming soon."

"Just think!" said Alison. "This blanket may keep some poor wounded soldier warm."

"It may save his life," Linda added.

All the girls looked at the blanket again.

"I'm *sure* it will win the prize," said Molly.

The girls folded the blanket as carefully as if it were a flag. "I'll wrap it in paper so it won't get dirty on the way to school," said Alison. She turned to Molly. "A blanket was a good idea, Molly. We couldn't have done it without you. Are you sure . . . I mean, what about your other project? Could we all help you with that?"

Molly looked down at her feet. "It isn't such a great project," she said. "Not like the blanket."

"And we weren't doing too well anyway," said Linda.

"What was it?" asked Grace.

Susan, Molly, and Linda looked at one another. They all smiled.

"Oh, it was *terrible*," said Susan. "We were collecting bottletops for scrap metal, and we knocked on everybody's door. It was so hard. We only got sixteen, and then we decided to come over here and sp—I mean, come over and see what you were doing."

"Collecting bottletops is a good project," said Alison. "I'll go ask my mother if she has any."

"If we all ask our mothers, we can get pretty many," said another girl.

"We wanted to get one hundred," said Linda.

"You know what?" said Grace. Her face was shiny and excited. "I live in an apartment building. There are twenty families in my building. We can ask all of them. I bet we'll get a hundred bottletops easily!"

"Yes, and we won't get wet!" laughed Molly. "Let's go!"

"We only need seventy-eight more," said Alison. "My mother had six!" She put the bottletops in Molly's school bag.

Molly smiled at her. "Thanks, Alison!" she said. Alison smiled, too.

With a flurry of buckling, zipping, buttoning, and tying, the ten girls got into their raincoats, boots, and rain hats. They set off for Grace's apartment building. As they splashed down the wet street, laughing and talking and planning, Molly decided that some secrets are a lot more fun when you give them away than when you keep them.

★ A Winning Spirit ★

Two days later, Molly cut an article out of the Jefferson Daily News to send to Dad.

THIRD-GRADE GIRLS
WIN LEND-A-HAND CONTEST

Ten students at Willow Street School showed the true meaning of allied effort this weekend. The third grade girls won first prize in the school's contest to help the war effort. They knitted a blanket and collected 100 bottletops, which they made into a sign saying "Lend a Hand."

"Both projects were a surprise to me," said their teacher, Miss Charlotte Campbell. "I don't know how the girls managed to finish them in one day. I am very proud of every one of the girls." At a school assembly today, each girl was given a blue ribbon.

The blanket will be sent to a hospital in England, where Dr. James McIntire, the father of Molly McIntire, is working with the U.S. Army Medical Corps. The bottletops will be given to the Boy Scouts' scrap metal drive.

The article included a photograph of all the girls,

along with Miss Campbell, holding the blanket. *Wait until Dad sees this*, Molly thought as she slipped the article into an envelope. Not only was the hospital in England getting a new blanket, they were getting a *blue ribbon* blanket at that!

A Different Christmas

 ecember 21
Dear Dad,
   Merry Christmas! How are you? I am fine
except I wish you would somehow magically be home for
Christmas. Do you have a Christmas tree in the hospital?
I hope so. Gram and Granpa are bringing our Christmas tree
tomorrow. I hope it's a big one! Right now, Mom is making
a wreath for the front door and Ricky and Brad are listen-
ing to the radio. Jill is knitting. I hope you got the presents
we sent you. We haven't gotten any presents from you yet.
Probably they will come soon. XOXOXOX

"Hey," Jill said. "I don't think you should write that."

Molly stopped making X's and O's on her letter and turned around. Jill was behind her, lounging sideways across Dad's chair, her legs dangling over one arm. She was reading the letter over Molly's shoulder.

"Write what?" asked Molly.

"That part about how we haven't gotten any presents from him."

"Why not?"

Jill swung her legs up and down. "Because," she said in a very patient voice, "Christmas is only four days away. By the time Dad gets that letter, Christmas will be over. If he didn't send us any presents—"

"But he did! I'm sure he did," said Molly. "Dad would never forget to send us Christmas presents."

Jill continued. "If he *didn't* send us any presents, he'll feel bad when he gets your letter. But by then it will be too late for him to do anything about it. And if he did send us presents, he'll feel bad because we never got them." She turned to her mother. "Don't you think I'm right, Mom?"

Mrs. McIntire was tying a bright red bow on the pine wreath. "I think it is Molly's letter and she should write whatever she wants to write."

Jill shrugged. She started to knit again.

Brad piped up. "Maybe Dad's present was on

a plane that got shot down by the Germans and drowned in the ocean."

"That's possible," said Ricky. Ricky considered himself an expert on fighter planes. "Those guys try to shoot down anything that flies." He took aim with an imaginary machine gun and fired at an imaginary plane. "POW! POW! POW!"

Brad looked up at his mother. "Will the Germans shoot down Santa's sleigh?"

"Of course not!" said Mrs. McIntire. She rumpled Brad's hair. "I'm sure Santa will get here safe and sound."

"I hope so," said Brad. "And I sure hope he brings me a soldier's hat and a real canteen."

"We'll just have to wait and see what Santa brings," said Mrs. McIntire. She stood up and took Brad's hand. "Come on. You can help me hang the wreath on the door. Then it's time for bed. Tomorrow is a big day. Gram and Granpa are going to bring us our Christmas tree."

As they walked into the hall together, Mrs. McIntire began, "'Twas the night before . . ."

"Christmas!" Brad ended.

"And all through the . . ."

"House!"

"Not a creature was . . ."

"Stirring!"

"Not even a . . ."

"Mouse!"

When they were gone, Jill stopped knitting. "Boy, I feel sorry for Brad," she said.

"Why?" asked Molly.

"For lots of reasons," said Jill. She tapped the palm of her hand with a knitting needle as she listed each reason. "First of all, Dad's gone. It hardly seems like Christmas without Dad here. And on top of that, there are no presents from him."

"Yet," corrected Molly. "No presents from Dad *yet*."

Jill ignored the interruption. "Then there's this Santa Claus business. Brad will be so disappointed when all he gets from Santa are boring presents like socks and handkerchiefs. It's not so bad for us. We're old enough not to mind. But he's still just a little kid. He wants that hat and canteen so badly. He won't understand why he can't have them." Jill stabbed her knitting needle into the ball of yarn.

"You mean he's not going to get them?" asked
Molly.

Ricky sat up. "Real soldiers need hats and can-
teens," he said. "They don't have any to spare."

Molly had an uncomfortable feeling that Jill and
Ricky were right.

"Besides," said Jill, "you know how Mom believes
it's not patriotic to spend money on unnecessary things
like toys. I'm sure all our presents this year will be
homemade or hand-me-downs." She stretched and
yawned. "I'm just glad there's nothing I really, really
want, so I won't be disappointed."

"But that's not true," said Molly. "You really want
a skating hat like the one you're making for Dolores,
don't you?"

"Sure, I do," said Jill. "So I've been saving my babysitting money to buy one for myself. I know that's the
only way I'll get it. It's childish to expect surprises this
Christmas."

"But remember what Dad used to say?" said Molly.
"There are *always* surprises at Christmas."

"This year is different," said Jill. "This is wartime.

There just won't be any wonderful surprises this Christmas. We have to be realistic."

"Realistic" was one of Jill's new words. It always sounded gloomy to Molly. Being realistic meant expecting things to be ordinary and dull. Molly did not want to feel that way about Christmas. And suddenly, Molly did not want to be part of this conversation anymore.

She stood up and put her letter to Dad in her pocket. "Well, I think I'm going to bed now." She hurried out of the room before Jill could say anything else realistic, and ran up the stairs two at a time.

Molly closed the door to her room. She sat on the window seat and looked out at the night. It was very dark. The black sky seemed to push up against her window. There were no stars to pin it back where it belonged. Molly hugged her knees to her chest and thought about what Jill had said. She knew Jill was right about one thing at least. It would be a simple Christmas. She should expect practical presents—things she really needed rather than things she dreamed about.

Molly hugged her knees tighter. She didn't *need* the

present she wanted more than anything else: a doll. Not a baby doll, but a doll she could have adventures with. Jill would say it was childish and unpatriotic to want something as unnecessary as a doll. And Molly knew it was certainly unrealistic to hope for a doll. But she couldn't help it. She couldn't stop hoping that by some magic, some Christmas magic, a new doll would be under the tree for her on Christmas morning. She couldn't stop hoping that the magic would bring something from Dad, too.

Because Dad loved Christmas. It was his favorite time of year. Right after Thanksgiving he would begin singing Christmas carols. Sometimes he would change the words to make Molly laugh. He would sing:

> *Deck the halls with boughs of holly,*
> *Fa-la-lu-la-la, la la la-la.*
> *'Tis the season to be Molly,*
> *Fa-la-la-la-la, la-la-la-la!*

Every year Dad made funny presents, too, and wrapped them in green tissue paper. No one could wait to open his surprises on Christmas morning. One year he made everyone—even Mom—a kite. The next year everyone got a yo-yo. Molly took her letter to Dad out of her pocket. Should she cross out the part about the presents? Maybe this year Dad was too busy to think of Christmas surprises. Things were probably very realistic where Dad was, in the middle of fighting. Molly sighed.

Just then there was a knock on the door and Molly's mother poked her head in. Her hand was covering her eyes. "May I come in? Or is this Santa's workshop? I don't want to see any presents before I'm supposed to."

Molly smiled. "It's okay, Mom. All my presents are already wrapped and hidden away."

Mom sat down on the window seat. "You're just like your father. His presents are always wrapped and ready before anyone else's."

"Not this year," said Molly. "I'm beginning to think maybe there won't be any presents from Dad this year. Maybe it's wrong to keep hoping."

"Now, Molly. Don't tell me you've given up on Dad."

"I don't know," said Molly slowly. "I want to think that a present will come. There is still enough time before Christmas. But . . ." Molly stopped. She looked down at her letter to Dad. The Christmas tree she had drawn was a little cockeyed. "But Jill says we have to be realistic. She says the war has made this Christmas different."

Mrs. McIntire reached over and smoothed Molly's bangs. "This Christmas *will* be different, Molly. Jill is right. We do have to be realistic about some things. We can't pretend there's no war. We can't pretend Dad is home. We can't ignore what's real."

"But I want Christmas to be special," said Molly. "I want Christmas to be full of surprises the way it is when Dad is home."

"So do I," said her mother. "And this Christmas can be special, but it will be up to us to make it special. If Dad can't be here to make our surprises for us, we'll just have to make them for ourselves." She grinned at Molly. "I think everyone in the McIntire family is pretty good at making surprises. I know I have a few surprises up my sleeve, and I bet you do, too." She leaned over and gave Molly a quick kiss on the forehead. "But it's never wrong to keep hoping for good things to happen, Molly, especially at Christmastime. That's what

Christmas is all about—hope." As she turned to close the door behind her, she said, "Good night, dear. Don't forget to brush your teeth before you go to bed."

"Good night, Mom," said Molly. She leaned her forehead against the cool windowpane. There were no stars to wish on. So she closed her eyes and made her wish deep inside herself. "I hope Dad's presents come. And I hope there will be lots of wonderful surprises this Christmas."

Making Surprises

olly's nose was tickled awake by a spicy smell. She sat up and took a deep breath. *Mmmm, cinnamon,* she thought. *Mom must be making sticky buns as a surprise for breakfast.* Molly grinned. She remembered what Mom had said the night before about making their own surprises. It looked—or rather, it smelled—as if Mom's surprises were already off to a delicious start.

Molly rolled out of bed and pulled on old corduroys and a flannel shirt. They had a nice, soft, easy, vacationy feeling. In them, Molly was ready for something unusual to happen. *If only I had a doll,* she thought as she pulled on a pair of thick socks. *This is just the kind of day when we would have an adventure together. Maybe we'd pretend to be ambulance drivers, or scientists cooking up some interesting concoction . . .*

Molly hurried into her shoes. The only concoction that interested her right now was being cooked up downstairs in the kitchen. She'd better hurry before Ricky ate up all the sticky buns.

She bounced down the stairs to the kitchen. But Ricky wasn't there. "Good morning, Mom," said Molly. "Where's Ricky?"

"He's already in the living room," Mrs. McIntire said. "He's moving furniture to make room for the Christmas tree."

Just as Molly bit into the warm, sweet bun, Ricky appeared at her elbow. "Hurry up and eat that," he said in a businesslike voice. "I need you to help me bring up the ornaments."

Molly's mouth was too full to answer, so she nodded her head eagerly. Ricky waited impatiently as she chewed and swallowed, gulped some milk, and wiped her sticky fingers. "Let's go," he commanded.

Molly followed Ricky down the dark steep steps to the cellar. There was only one light behind them, a bare bulb hanging at the top of the stairs. Their shadows danced before them like cheerful ghosts. They seemed to say, "Here you are at last! We've been waiting all year for you to come down and open this closet! Now the fun can begin!"

Molly jumped ahead of Ricky and pulled open the closet door. Every Christmas she could remember had begun the same way. Dad would open this door—the door to the Christmas closet—and say, "Ho, ho, ho! What have we here?"

The closet was full of Christmas. It smelled of dried pine needles, mothballs, crushed peppermint candy canes, and bayberry-scented candles. Bags overflowed with curlicued ribbons, paper chains, rolls of wrapping paper, and shiny strands of tinsel. Boxes of Christmas tree ornaments were piled in shaky stacks, waiting to be carried upstairs and dusted off, so they could shine in the light and work their Christmas magic again. Molly was glad to see them. She scooped up an armload and held the boxes steady with her chin.

Ricky pulled a string of Christmas tree lights off the shelf. "I'll take care of these this year," he said.

Molly was doubtful. No one but Dad had ever handled the lights before. The tangled string of lights looked like a thorny vine. "Do you think you can do it?" she asked. "Even Dad has trouble . . ."

"Don't worry, fussbudget. I can figure these out," Ricky said. He slung the loop of lights over his shoulder and marched up the stairs.

Molly climbed the stairs behind him. With every step she took, a bell jingled in one of the boxes she carried. "Ho, ho, ho!" she said as she jiggled the box to make the bell ring louder. "Here comes Christmas!"

Brad ran to meet her at the top of the stairs. "Oh! Let me see!" he cried. "Where's my stocking?" Molly lowered her pile of boxes to the floor and knelt down to open them.

"Hey, look!" Brad held up a battered star cut out of cardboard and covered with wrinkled tinfoil. "Here's the star I made last year."

Jill sat at the kitchen table calmly eating a sticky bun with a fork. She glanced down at the boxes scattered on the floor. "Uh, *honestly*," she said with a scowl. "Did you have to haul all that stuff out of the basement?"

Molly looked up. "But these are the Christmas tree ornaments. We need them."

Jill raised her eyebrows, then turned back to her sticky bun. "They're so . . . junky. I think this year we should use only store-bought balls, none of those homemade ornaments or messy paper chains."

No one said anything.

Jill touched her lips with her napkin. "And I think we should use only blue and red balls and blue and red lights. It will look patriotic."

Molly thought that was a terrible idea. "But we don't have very many blue and red balls," she said.

"We don't need many," said Jill. "We usually put too much junk on the tree anyway. It will look more elegant with just a few balls."

Brad looked down at his tinfoil star.

"I don't want the tree to look *elegant*," said Molly. "I want it to look—"

"Just like last year," interrupted Jill. "I know. You want everything to be just like last year. And I keep telling you it just can't be."

Ricky put the string of lights on the table. "What do you think, Mom?" he asked.

Mrs. McIntire put her hands in the pockets of her apron. "Well, I think it would be nice to have an elegant, patriotic tree. But I know I would miss all the old ornaments. They're like old friends." She thought for a moment. "How about this? I saw a picture in a magazine of a Christmas tree with a flag on top instead of an angel or a star. It looked very patriotic. What if we used all of our old ornaments but put a flag at the top of our tree?"

"That would be good!" said Brad.

Molly looked at Jill. "What do you think, Jill?"

Jill shrugged. "Frankly, I don't really care. It was just a suggestion." She stepped over the boxes of ornaments and walked to the sink to wash her plate.

"Well!" said Mom in a cheerful voice. "That's settled! Brad and I are going downtown today anyway. We'll just add a flag to our shopping list."

Right after breakfast, Mom and Brad got ready to go out. Brad's pockets were so full of pennies he'd saved for buying presents that he clanked when he walked. "You sound like a walking piggy bank," said Jill.

As Mrs. McIntire put on her coat, she said, "We'll have lunch in town. But we'll be back before Gram and Granpa get here with the Christmas tree."

No sooner had Mom and Brad disappeared from sight than the phone rang. Ricky was on his hands and knees trying to untangle a string of lights stretched across the living room. "It's probably for you, Jill," he said. "It almost always is."

Jill picked up the telephone. "Hello? Oh, hello, Grammy!" she said with a smile. "No, Mom's not here. She and Brad are shopping."

As Ricky and Molly watched, Jill's smile sank into a worried frown. "Oh," she said. "Oh, that's too bad. Can't you get it fixed? Oh." She turned away so they could only see her back. "Yes, I'll tell Mom. Well, we'll . . . we'll certainly miss you. No, no presents have come from Dad yet. I'll tell Mom to call if a box arrives. Well, we're sorry, too. Say hello to Granpa for us. Good-bye." She hung up.

"What happened?" asked Molly. "What's the matter?"

Jill turned around. "They can't come," she stated.

"What?" gasped Ricky and Molly together.

"Grammy says they had a flat tire. Their spare tire is too old to use on such a long trip. So they'll have to wait and get the other tire patched. No one can do it until after the weekend. So," she repeated grimly, "they can't come."

"Oh, no!" wailed Molly. She sat down on the floor next to a box of ornaments.

"Oh, boy. What a Christmas!" said Ricky glumly. "First no Dad. Now no Gram and Granpa."

"And no *tree*," said Molly. "No Christmas tree from Gram and Granpa's farm."

"Well, what do we need a tree for anyway?" asked Ricky. He kicked away a string of lights with his foot. "We don't have any presents from Dad to put under it."

"We have our presents for each other," Molly said weakly.

"Big deal," said Ricky.

Molly began to feel as gloomy as she had the night before. "I wish Mom were here," she said.

"Mom couldn't do anything about it," said Ricky. "Let's face it. This Christmas is ruined. No one can do anything about it."

Molly thought about what Mom had told her last night. "Mom says we have to rely on ourselves this Christmas. She says *we* have to make Christmas special this year."

"What are we supposed to do?" asked Ricky. "Make a Christmas tree?"

Jill had been very quiet, but now she said, "We could buy a tree. We could do that ourselves."

"How?" said Ricky. "I only have twenty-five cents left."

"I have money," said Jill.

"But that's your babysitting money," said Molly. "I thought you were saving that for—"

"A tree is more important," Jill interrupted. "Come on. Let's hurry. Let's get the tree before Mom and Brad get home."

"Wait a minute," said Molly. She ran upstairs, rummaged in the closet, then ran downstairs again. "Here," she panted. She showed Jill a lumpy package wrapped in red paper. "This is—this *was* my Christmas present for Brad. It's fifty pennies. We may need it."

Jill nodded briskly. "Good," she said. "Now we have plenty."

Jill led the way. Molly and Ricky hurried to catch up. "But where will we get a tree?" asked Ricky as he stumbled along, trying to button up his jacket.

"Boy Scouts are selling trees at the school," said Jill. "Hurry up."

The Boy Scouts had created a small forest of pines

in a corner of the school playground. Molly, Jill, and Ricky walked through it slowly, examining each tree carefully. Finally, Jill stopped. "This is it," she said.

Molly looked at the tree. It was tall and skinny. There were so many gaps between branches that it looked like a comb with most of its teeth missing. "This one?" she asked. "But—"

Ricky jabbed her with his elbow. He pointed to the price tag. Suddenly, Molly understood. This was the only tree they could afford to buy.

Jill gave all of her babysitting money to the Boy Scout in charge. Ricky handed him his twenty-five cents. Molly poured fifty pennies into the Boy Scout's hands. They each grabbed on to the trunk of the tree and headed home.

"Well, at least it's not heavy," said Ricky.

Molly looked at the tree. It was scrawny. But it had the sharp pine scent that meant Christmas. Molly broke off a needle and bit it. A bitter piney tang filled her mouth. "Let's decorate the tree before Mom and Brad get home," she said. "That way it will be a great surprise for them."

Jill shook her head. "You and your surprises," she

said. But Molly could tell Jill was excited, too, because she began to walk a little faster. The tree bounced with every step.

This tree is going to be okay, Molly thought as they hurried home in the pale December sunshine. *Mom and Brad will be so surprised. And we did it all by ourselves.* Molly grinned. *I guess Mom was right. All the McIntires are pretty good at surprises.*

It was dark before dinnertime. Molly and Jill were lying on the living room floor, gazing up through the branches of the decorated Christmas tree. Once the lights and ornaments were on it, the tree did not look scrawny at all. In fact, Molly thought it looked beautiful.

"Jill, do you mind that we put all the old ornaments on the tree?" she asked. "Are you disappointed that it's not elegant?"

"No," said Jill. "This tree *needed* all the ornaments. Besides, I didn't really like that idea of only red and blue balls. I just thought it might be better if the tree looked different this year." She sighed. "See, when everything looks the same as last year, it just makes me miss Dad even more. Everything is the same except for one big, horrible difference—Dad isn't here."

"Oh," said Molly. "I never thought of it that way." She looked up at the colored lights wound around the tree. They looked like shining jewels on the green branches. "Well, I think this is the most beautiful Christmas tree we've ever had."

Jill smiled. "You say that every year."

"I know," said Molly. "But this year it's true. Even Mom said so."

Molly and Jill were happily quiet. They were both thinking of when Mom and Brad had come home to the glittering tree. Molly had never seen her mother so completely surprised. She shivered with pleasure when she recalled Mom's pleased, proud face.

"You know what, Jill? I'm beginning to think that making surprises for other people is more fun than getting surprises yourself."

"Mmmm," said Jill.

Molly couldn't tell if Jill was listening or not, but she went on. "I mean, it will still be great to get Dad's surprises, of course."

Jill tapped one of the dangling balls so that it swung back and forth like the pendulum of a clock.

"How come you're still so sure we'll get presents from Dad?" she asked.

Molly was silent for a moment. Should she say out loud the worry she had been carrying around for days? She took a deep breath. "Oh, Jill," Molly said, "I have to keep thinking a package will come, because if it doesn't I'm scared it means . . ." She stopped.

Jill rolled onto her side. "If nothing comes, it means Dad may be hurt or sick or lost. It means maybe he *couldn't* send any presents."

Molly nodded. It was kind of a relief to know that Jill shared the same heavy worry.

"It's not really the presents I care about," said Molly. "I just hope a box or something—even a card or a letter—will come so we'll know Dad is okay."

"I know what you mean," said Jill. "I'm worried about exactly the same thing."

Molly looked up through the tangle of branches. Brad's tinfoil star was near the top of the tree, next to a yellow light. *Please let Dad be okay*, Molly wished. The tinfoil star seemed to twinkle just like a real star that was trying to reassure her. Molly wondered if Jill saw it, too.

Keeping Secrets

omething wonderful had happened. Molly knew it the minute she woke up. Her room was full of sunshine. Light shimmered and danced on the walls. Molly pushed back the covers and hurried out of bed. The floor was cold to her bare feet, so she hopped from rug to rug as if they were stepping-stones across an icy stream. She looked out the window. SNOW. Beautiful, perfect, bright white snow all over everything, as thick as icing on a cake.

Oh, boy, snow! thought Molly. She couldn't wait to get outside into all that deep, clean whiteness.

Molly didn't stop to get dressed. With her socks and shoes in hand, she rushed across the hall and burst into Jill's room. Jill was snuggled so deep under the covers that only the top of her head showed. Her hair was bobby-pinned in rows of tight curls, and her head looked like a prickly pineapple resting on the pillow.

Molly shook her shoulder. "Jill!" she whispered urgently. "Wake up!"

Jill rolled over and opened one eye. "What?"

"Come on. Get up. It *snowed*." Molly wobbled on one foot, pulling a sock on the other foot as she talked.

"Ohhhhh," Jill moaned. "Go away."

"But Jill," said Molly, "it's the first snow of the winter. Don't you want to go out and—"

"No!" Jill snapped. "I want to sleep. I can't believe you woke me up just because of some stupid snow. Now go away." She pulled the covers over her head.

Molly backed out of Jill's room and closed the door. Last year, Jill woke Molly up the first time it snowed. She was just as excited as Molly was. They made outlines of angels all over the driveway by lying on their backs in the snow and moving their arms up and down. Molly sighed. She should have realized Jill wouldn't care about the snow this year. Now that Jill was fourteen, she didn't get excited about anything that was fun anymore. She was *realistic*.

Molly tiptoed downstairs to the kitchen. She pulled on her snow jacket, boots, hat, and mittens and went outside. The whole world was blue sky and white snow. It was as if Molly had stepped out of her same old back door into an enchanted land no one had ever seen or touched before. It was hers alone. Yesterday the trees were sad, scrawny black skeletons. Today their branches were soft white arms opened wide, outstretched to welcome the snow. Everything was smoothed and softened by the sparkling blanket of white.

With a wild whoop, Molly took a flying leap off the stairs into a drift of snow. It was like jumping into a cloud. A car made its way slowly down the street, its tire chains jingling like bells on a sleigh.

The snow came to the top of Molly's boots. She scooped up a handful to lick. *Snow for Christmas,* she thought. *It's perfect. It's a great big giant Christmas surprise. Now the whole entire world will be ready for Christmas.* She wondered what Dad's Christmas would be like in England. Maybe the fighting would stop for a while. The doctors and nurses in the hospital might have a Christmas party. Would they sing Christmas carols and give each other presents?

Molly wished she were old enough to be a Red

Cross nurse. Then she could go to England and work in the hospital with Dad. She'd wear a uniform as white as this morning's snow and a cap with a red cross on it. "Nurse McIntire," that's what the soldiers would call her. She'd ride in the ambulance out to the battlefields and rescue the poor wounded soldiers while guns fired all around her. Nothing would scare her. Nothing would stop her, not blizzards, or bombs, or—WHACK! Something cold and wet hit Molly on the leg. It was a snowball!

"Bombs away!" yelled Ricky from his bedroom window. He launched another snowball at Molly.

"Cut it out," Molly laughed. She threw a handful of snow up at him. Ricky had made a stockpile of balls from the snow around his windows. Molly ran and dodged as he pelted her with snowball after snowball.

Ricky imitated the deep voice radio announcers used when they described American airplanes bombing the enemy: "Our brave fliers! Bombers who can hit (Smack!) any target with deadly accuracy. (Whack!) Nothing can stop these Flying Fortresses from (Got ya!) delivering their tons and tons of bombs. (Bam!)"

Suddenly Jill appeared on the back steps. "Richard

Culver McIntire!" she said in her bossiest voice. "Close that window immediately. You'll freeze the entire house."

Ricky chucked his last snowball at Jill and then vanished. Molly looked at her sister. "I thought you wanted to sleep."

Jill grinned back and shrugged. "I figured I was already awake. I might as well come out."

"Let's go make angels in the front yard," said Molly.

"Okay," said Jill. Her cheeks were already as red as Christmas bows.

Molly made a chain of neat bootprints in a single line around the corner of the house. Jill stepped in the prints Molly made. They always liked to leave the snow as pure and unmarked as possible.

"Our house looks as perfect as an old-fashioned Christmas card, doesn't it?" Molly sighed as she looked up at Mom's wreath on the front door. Suddenly, she stopped walking. What was that lump on the front porch, right under the wreath? She began to run, slipping and sliding across the smooth white yard, stumbling up the steps to the front door. She dropped to her knees on the top step.

"Jill!" she said. "Come quick!" She began digging wildly at the lump, sending the snow whirling in a small blizzard.

"What is it?" asked Jill. Then she saw it, too—a box as big as a suitcase, half buried in the snow.

Molly brushed the snow off the top of the box. Jill read the label:

> *FROM:*
> *CAPT. J. MCINTIRE*
> *U.S. ARMY MEDICAL CORPS*
> *APO 299*
>
> *TO:*
> *THE MERRY MCINTIRES*
> *467 OAK STREET*
> *JEFFERSON, ILLINOIS*
> *USA*

"It's from Dad! It's from Dad!" said Molly. She felt happiness exploding inside her like fireworks. She hugged the box as if it were her father. "Come on! Let's dig it out and go show everybody. Wait until they see!"

Jill was too happy to talk. She sat right down on the steps and helped Molly clear the snow away from the box. The brown paper was torn and ragged, spotted with stamps and stickers.

Molly dug all the snow away from one end of the box. There, in big letters, was a message. It said: *KEEP HIDDEN UNTIL CHRISTMAS DAY!*

It was Dad's handwriting. Molly would know it anywhere. It was as familiar as his face. Molly could almost hear her father's voice saying those words. The voice would be full of fun, but serious, too.

"Jill, look at this." Molly pointed to the words.

Jill read the message. "Keep hidden . . ." she whispered.

"Dad wants us to hide the box until Christmas. That's two days away," said Molly.

Jill frowned. "I don't know if we *should* hide it. I'm so glad it's here, because it means Dad is okay. I want to tell everyone, but . . ." She read the message again.

Molly stood up. "Let's put it away somewhere first, then decide what to do."

Jill nodded. "Okay."

Like two excited pirates feverishly digging up a long-lost treasure, Jill and Molly pulled the box out of the snow.

"Where should we put it?" asked Jill. "We can't take it into the house."

"The garage. We'll put it in the storage room above the garage," said Molly.

Jill took one end of the box and Molly took the other, and they walked to the corner of the house. Molly craned her neck around to look up at Ricky's windows. They were closed. "The coast is clear," she said.

Jill made a face. "This box is so heavy my arms are being pulled out of their sockets," she said. "There must be lots of great presents inside." Her carefully bobby-pinned curls hung in bedraggled clumps.

The girls waddled across the driveway as quickly as they could. The box pushed against their stomachs, making it hard to breathe. Step, thump! Step, thump! They struggled up the stairs to the room above the garage. Molly pushed the door open. Once inside, they put the box down and collapsed like melted snowmen.

"Phew! That was hard," said Jill. She leaned back against the door.

Molly was sweating under her snow jacket. Bobbles of snow were frozen on her pajama legs. Her hands inside her mittens were stiff with cold and from the weight of the box.

Molly and Jill stared at the box.

"So what do you think is in there?" asked Jill.

"Presents, of course."

"Yes, but what?" Jill squatted next to the box. She smoothed the wet brown wrapping paper. "Maybe we should open it up, just to be sure nothing is broken or anything."

"No peeking," said Molly. "That's not fair. Dad wants everything about this box to be a surprise."

Jill looked sheepish. She sat down again. "But Dad doesn't know how worried we've been. He doesn't know what it's been like to wait and wait and wait for even a letter. He doesn't know how much we've been hoping for this box."

Molly smiled. "I thought you were being *realistic* about Christmas this year. I thought you said it was childish to hope for surprises."

Jill laughed. "I guess I did. But I guess I really never stopped hoping this box would come. That's why I think we should tell everybody about it right away. They're all hoping, too. It would make them so happy."

"But Dad said to keep it hidden until Christmas Day," Molly answered. "If we tell everyone now, we'll ruin his surprise."

Jill thought a moment. Then she stood up. "Okay. We'd better hide it in the corner, in case someone comes up here."

Molly and Jill pushed the box into the darkest corner of the room. Molly pulled a dusty old blanket over it, and then put two broken tennis rackets on top.

"There!" she said as she backed away. "That ought to do it."

The box under the blanket looked like a lumpy brown bear sleeping peacefully in a corner. "I don't want to go away and leave it," said Jill. "I'm afraid it's a dream and the box will be gone when we come back."

"I know what you mean," said Molly. "But we'd better go. Everybody will be getting up for breakfast. We can check on the box later."

Jill nudged the box with the toe of her boot. "Good old Dad," she said.

"I *told* you he wouldn't forget," said Molly. "Come on. Let's go. And remember to act as if nothing has happened."

As she followed Jill down the stairs and across the driveway, Molly felt happy—completely, entirely, head-to-toe happy. She and Jill stamped their feet at the back door to make the snow avalanche off their boots. When they went into the kitchen, Mrs. McIntire took one look at them and laughed. "Well, you two look like rosy little elves! Where have you been? Up to the North Pole working on Santa's surprises for all of us?"

Molly felt her face get hot. Mom's joke was too close to the truth. She stooped over to unbuckle her boots. "We were just out—outside," she stammered.

"Playing in the snow," finished Jill.

"So I see," said Mrs. McIntire. She lifted Molly's wet hat off her head with two fingers. "How did you manage to get dirt streaked across your jacket when everything is covered with snow?"

Molly looked down at her jacket. Dust from the old blanket had left a trail across it. She didn't know what to say.

"We were in the garage," said Jill, in a voice as cool and light as a snowflake.

"Looking for the sleds, I'll bet," Mrs. McIntire smiled. "Well, you can go sledding all you like after breakfast. But right now, both of you scoot upstairs and put on dry clothes. Molly, you're still in your pajamas!"

Molly and Jill galloped up the stairs. At the top, Jill yanked Molly into her room and closed the door.

"Phew!" said Molly. "I thought maybe she saw us with the box or something."

"Listen," said Jill. "I think we should tell Mom about the box. Dad probably thought she'd be the one to get it first anyway."

"It *would* be easier if she knew," admitted Molly. "It almost feels like we're lying to her by keeping it a secret."

"That's what I think, too," said Jill. "Besides, she's probably suspicious. You're terrible at this secret-keeping business. You're acting as if you robbed a bank or something. Mom must know you have a secret."

"Well, everybody has secrets at Christmastime," said Molly.

"Yeah, but not as big as this one," said Jill. "Let's tell Mom about the box."

But Molly just couldn't give in. "Telling one person is the same as telling everyone. You can't keep a secret just a little bit. You either keep it completely or give it all away. Dad wants to surprise everyone for Christmas. We have to help him."

Jill crossed her arms. "All right, all right. But how much longer do we have to keep the box hidden?"

Molly thought. "We'll have to wait until everyone goes to sleep on Christmas Eve. Then we'll sneak out to the garage and get it and put it under the tree. But until then, absolutely no telling anyone—not Mom, not Brad, *nobody*. Promise?"

"Okay, I promise," said Jill. She grinned. "Now I know how Santa Claus must feel."

Molly grinned, too. "It's not easy to keep Christmas surprises a secret," she said. "But this one is worth it. This will be the best Christmas surprise anyone has ever had."

The Merry McIntires

eeping Dad's secret did not get any easier for Molly. She was jittery all day Saturday. After breakfast, when Brad rushed to the garage to get his sled, Molly planted herself like a guard at the bottom of the stairs to the storage room. Jill rolled her eyes at her and hissed, "Move away!" Molly wouldn't budge. What if Brad went up to the storage room? What if he saw the box? But Brad was interested only in his sled. He didn't even notice Molly.

There was another alarm after lunch when Ricky went to the garage to get a snow shovel. Molly hovered around him so much that Ricky finally gave her a shovel and told her to help out. Molly didn't mind shoveling the driveway. At least she could keep an eye on the garage without looking suspicious that way.

By the end of the day, Molly was exhausted. This

secret-keeping business was hard work. And there was still one whole day to get through—one more nerve-racking day—until she and Jill could reveal the surprise.

The next day was Christmas Eve. Molly was on pins and needles all morning. Luckily, Mom was up in her room until noon, wrapping presents. She couldn't see the garage from there. And Ricky and Brad built a snow fort in the front yard. They spent the morning cheerfully bombarding each other with snowballs.

At last it was time for everyone to get ready to go to church for the Christmas Eve service. As Molly put on her special green velvet Christmas dress, she felt relieved. The secret would be safe while they were all at church.

Molly loved the Christmas Eve service. The church was decorated with red and white poinsettias and gar-lands of pine and holly. A dark manger scene filled the front of the church. Everyone was given a small white candle to hold. The flame of Molly's candle flickered and danced as she listened to the words of the Christmas story:

*And suddenly there was with the Angel
a multitude of heavenly hosts praising
God and saying, "Glory to God in the
highest, and on earth, peace, good will
toward men."*

Molly knew everyone in her family was thinking of Dad and hoping this Christmas would truly bring peace on earth so that he could come home.

Maybe next Christmas Dad will be here with us, thought Molly. She remembered how his deep voice sang out, "Silent night, holy night." Molly looked down the pew. She saw a tear caught like a tiny diamond in the corner of her mother's eye, shining in the light of the candle. Molly bit her lip. *Maybe we should have told her about the box,* she thought. *Maybe then she wouldn't be so sad.*

But when they walked home from church, Mom seemed happy. Their neighbors' calls of "Merry Christmas!" were warm in the snappy cold night.

They had their traditional Christmas Eve supper of scrambled eggs, bacon, hot chocolate, and cinnamon toast before they hung their stockings on the mantel.

Mom read *'Twas the Night Before Christmas* just as Dad read it every year. They all knew that the last line of the poem was their signal to go to bed. So everyone stood up and said with Mom, "Merry Christmas to all and to all a good night!" Then they ran up the stairs to their rooms and jumped into bed.

Tick, tock, tick, tock, Molly's heart thudded with every tick of the clock. She was waiting, waiting, waiting for it to be midnight. At midnight she and Jill would perform their secret mission. They would put Dad's box under the Christmas tree.

Molly opened her eyes very wide. Her room was solidly dark, filled corner to corner with blackness. She rolled over on her side and looked at her glow-in-the-dark clock for the millionth time. Only four minutes to go. She couldn't wait any longer. She sat up. Did her bed always creak so loudly? Slowly, carefully, she stood up and tiptoed to the door. Slowly, carefully, she opened it.

BAM! A white shape bumped into her. Molly gasped and the white shape giggled. It was Jill. She put her finger over her lips to signal "no talking." Molly put her slippers on her feet, and they both went into the hallway. They felt their way down the stairs in absolute darkness, putting two feet on each step like unsteady babies. Molly didn't even breathe until they got to the kitchen.

Jill headed to the closet to get her jacket. Molly grabbed her arm and whispered, "No! Too noisy!" All of a sudden, she felt sort of wobbly. She moved her hand down Jill's arm and Jill squeezed it. Molly felt better. She opened the back door and went outside.

The cold bit their skin. Quickly they dashed across the driveway, up the stairs, and into the storage room.

"This is kind of scary, isn't it?" Molly whispered.

"Oooh, I think it's fun," said Jill. "It's like a ghost story."

Molly shivered. "Come on. Let's hurry." They carried the box down the icy steps, across the driveway, through the kitchen, and into the living room, then put it under the tree. There were several tempting boxes that had not been there before. Molly pointed to them. "Santa Claus has been here," she said.

For some reason that made both Jill and Molly burst into giggles. They grabbed pillows from the sofa to muffle their laughter. When they finally quieted down, they crept up the stairs to bed. Jill waved good night outside her door. Molly waved back. *Mission accomplished,* thought Molly. She curled up under the covers, drowsy and happy and very, very relieved.

"MOM! MOM! MOM! MOM!" was the next thing Molly heard. She opened her eyes. The sun was just coming up and her room was rosy. "MOM!" she heard Brad call again as he thundered down the hall. "Merry Christmas! Get up!"

The McIntires had a rule that no one could go downstairs to the Christmas tree until everyone was ready. Brad banged on Jill's door, then Molly's door, then Ricky's door. When they were all gathered at the top of the stairs, Mrs. McIntire smiled and said, "Okay, go ahead!" Everyone stampeded down the stairs.

At the door of the living room, the stampede stopped suddenly. "Hey," said Brad, "what's that big box?"

Ricky rushed past him to the tree. "Mom!" he squeaked. "It's from Dad! Look, it's from Dad!"

Mrs. McIntire's face went white. "From . . . ?" she whispered. She knelt down next to the box and touched the label. She looked up. "It is! It's from your father! But how?" She looked at Jill and Molly. They smiled. Mrs. McIntire sat down on the floor.

"You two!" she laughed. "Why didn't you tell us about the box?"

"Dad said not to," said Molly. "Look." She pointed to Dad's message.

"Keep hidden . . ." Mrs. McIntire read. "Just like your father! Always surprises!" She hugged first Jill, then Molly. Molly could feel her trembling.

"Well, what are we waiting for?" said Ricky. "Let's open it." He tore the brown paper off the box and ripped open the lid.

"Oooh," said Brad. "Look!"

The box was filled with green tissue paper lumps in odd shapes and sizes. Each lump was labeled.

Ricky handed them out. "One for Brad. One for Jill. One for Molly. One for Mom. One for me."

Brad opened his bundle in no time. "A canteen," he said contentedly. "And a soldier's hat. I guess Santa asked Dad to get them."

Ricky had a silk scarf made from a genuine parachute—the kind real pilots wore. Jill had a heather-colored skating hat. "*Much* nicer than Dolores's," she said with satisfaction. Mom had buttery-smooth leather gloves. She slid her hands into the gloves and smiled as she pulled out a small white note. She seemed too happy to say anything.

"Oh, look!" cried Molly. Everyone knelt around her as she lifted her gift out of its rustling tissue paper. It was a beautiful doll with dark shiny hair and smiling blue eyes. Molly touched the doll's hair with one finger and traced the curve of her pink cheek. She was dressed in a nurse's uniform and hat like the one Molly had dreamed about. A smart red cape covered her starched dress and tied under her chin. Molly hugged her. This doll would be her companion in adventures, the secret sharer of all her dreams. When she played with her, Molly would always remember that Dad had chosen this doll for her. Even though he was far away, he still knew what would make Molly the happiest girl in the world. If only Dad could be there with them to see how happy his surprise had made them all.

"Well," said Mrs. McIntire suddenly. "What time do you think it is?"

"It's exactly seven-oh-three," said Ricky, who never took off his watch.

Mrs. McIntire glanced at the white note in her hand, then put it in her bathrobe pocket. "Let's turn on the radio," she said. "We can listen to the Christmas shows while we open the rest of our presents."

Ricky flicked on the radio. Christmas music filled the room. "Joy to the world!" the singers sang. The music was drowned out with whoops of delight as Brad and Ricky, Jill and Molly opened present after present. Molly was glad to see that not *all* the presents she got were so very practical. Jill gave her a glass ball that filled with snowflakes when she shook it, and Brad gave her a corsage he'd made out of pinecones and red ribbon.

All too soon, all the presents were unwrapped. Molly sat in a sea of crumpled wrapping paper, eating Christmas coffee cake. Brad insisted on drinking his juice out of his canteen. Ricky flung his scarf around his neck and pretended that he was the voice on the radio singing:

> *May your days be merry and bright,*
> *And may all your Christmases be white.*

Then a scratchy voice on the radio said, "Merry Christmas! We're broadcasting from the USO Christmas party in England, and we have some servicemen here with messages for the folks back home. Here's an eager fellow. What's your name, Captain?"

"I'm Captain James McIntire," said a familiar voice. They all stopped still and looked at the radio. "I'd like to say Merry Christmas to all the merry McIntires—Jill, Ricky, Molly, Brad, and my wife, Helen."

Molly held her doll very tight.

"I miss you all very much. And I hope you have a wonderful Christmas full of happy surprises."

And that was all. Other soldiers spoke, but Molly didn't hear them. She kept the echo of Dad's voice. She never wanted it to fade. Dad. What he said was still true. There *were* always surprises at Christmas.

INSIDE Molly's World

When Molly's story takes place, America had been fighting in World War Two for three long years. The war had been going on since 1939, when Germany attacked Poland, England, and France. Many Americans wanted to stay out of the war. It wasn't until 1941, when Japan bombed Pearl Harbor, a naval base in Hawaii, that Americans joined the fight.

Like Molly, children all over the world desperately missed their relatives who went to war. Almost every family in the United States had to say good-bye to someone. Thousands of American men volunteered to fight, becoming soldiers, pilots, and sailors. Some drove ambulances and tanks. Others worked as doctors, mechanics, and cooks. Women joined the armed forces, too. They worked in military hospitals and offices. They drove jeeps, ordered supplies, and nursed the wounded.

When American soldiers joined the fighting, American factories "went to war," too. Car factories made airplanes and tanks instead of new cars. Clothing factories made uniforms and tents instead of dresses. Factories that once made toys now made war equipment. Things like bicycles were almost impossible to get until the fighting was over.

Before the war, most American women did not have jobs. But as men went away to fight, women went to work in offices and factories. They built and tested airplanes, repaired train engines, and ran businesses.

Even people who did not go off to fight said they were "fighting on the home front." People in the United States changed the way they lived in order to help win the war. They drove their cars less so there would be plenty of gas for airplanes, tanks, and army trucks. They stopped buying food in cans so the metal could be used for guns and bullets. They raised their own food by planting Victory gardens so that the food farmers grew could go to the soldiers.

People on the home front also coped with shortages. Some things, like sugar and rubber, were scarce because the war was going on in the countries where sugar and rubber came from. Those items were *rationed*, which meant Americans could buy only small amounts of them.

Children did their part to help their country win the war, too. Every school had scrap drives and contests like the Lend-a-Hand Contest at Molly's school. In scrap drives, children collected old pots and pans, tinfoil, car tires, and other material that could be used to make war equipment. Children also belonged to the Junior Red Cross and other groups. They made food packages for soldiers, rolled bandages out of strips of cloth, and knitted sweaters, socks, and blankets for the fighting men.

World War Two was hard for the people who fought and for people on the home front. But Americans were willing to make the sacrifices they did because they believed that winning the war would make the world a better place for everyone.

Read more of MOLLY'S stories,

available from booksellers and at *americangirl.com*

❧ *Classics* ❧

Molly's classic series, now in two volumes:

Volume 1:
A Winning Spirit

Life on the home front is full of challenges. Molly does her best to make do with less and help the war effort. Missing Dad, who is far away in England, is the hardest sacrifice of all!

Volume 2:
Stars, Stripes, and Surprises

Even allies have arguments sometimes. Molly learns to get along with new friends as well as forever friends, with some surprises along the way.

❧ *Journey in Time* ❧

Travel back in time—and spend a day with Molly!

Chances and Changes

Take a trip to Camp Gowonagin with Molly! Go on an over night nature hike, compete in the swim meet, and discover fun camp traditions. Choose your own path through this multiple-ending story.

Parents, request a FREE catalogue at
americangirl.com/catalogue.
Sign up at **americangirl.com/email** to receive the latest news and exclusive offers.

A Sneak Peek at

Stars, Stripes, and Surprises

A Molly Classic

Volume 2

Molly's adventures continue in the
second volume of her classic stories.

olly McIntire was skipping rope at the end of her driveway on a blustery afternoon in early spring. She was waiting for her friends Linda and Susan. Molly had a very important piece of news to tell them. Oh, wait until they heard! Molly skipped a little faster, as if that would make them come sooner. The wind sent high white clouds hurrying across the sky. It pushed hard against Molly, too, but she wouldn't budge from her lookout post. Where *were* Linda and Susan? Molly stopped skipping. She shaded her eyes and peered down the street. They were supposed to come over right after lunch. Molly felt as if she had been waiting forever.

At last Molly saw her friends. Linda was walking quickly. She bent into the wind. Her hands were shoved deep in her pockets. She stopped from time to time to wait for Susan, who was much slower. Susan had one foot on the curb and one foot in the gutter, where she was carefully cracking the thin ice over winter's last puddles.

"Hurry up!" Molly called.

Linda poked Susan, and they both ran to Molly.

"Guess what! Guess what!" shouted Molly.

"What?" Linda and Susan puffed together.

"An English girl is coming to stay with us!" said Molly happily.

"Oooh!" breathed Susan.

"What do you mean?" asked Linda.

"A girl," said Molly, "from London. Her parents want her to come to America where it's safe. She's supposed to stay with her aunt here in Jefferson until the war's over. But her aunt has pneumonia or something and can't take her, so my mom said she could stay with us."

"Until the war is over?" asked Linda.

"No, just until her aunt gets better," said Molly. "But Mom said she'd be with us a few weeks at least, and that means she'll be here for my birthday."

"Oh, Molly," sighed Susan. "You're so lucky! A real English girl for your birthday!"

"I don't get it," said Linda. "Why is she coming *now*? England has been in the war a long time."

"Well," Molly thought out loud, "maybe her house was just bombed by the Nazis."

"And she's probably ragged and starving like the children in *Life* magazine pictures," added Susan.

Linda shook her head. "Not everyone in England is ragged and starving, Susan," she said. "For all you know, she's as rich as a princess."

"A princess!" said Susan joyfully.

"I bet she even looks like the English princesses, Margaret Rose or Elizabeth!" said Molly. "I bet she has dark curly hair and blue eyes. She's going to share my room and come to school with me. She's exactly our age."

"Does she know your dad in England?" asked Linda.

"No, I don't think so," answered Molly.

"When does she come?" asked Susan.

"Today!"

"Today!" shrieked Susan and Linda. "What time?"

"Mom said before dinner," Molly answered.

"Well, I'm not going to stand out here all day waiting for her," said Linda. She was holding her coat collar up around here ears. "I'm cold. Let's go inside."

"Maybe when the English girl is here, Mrs. Gilford will give us little tea sandwiches every afternoon, like they have in England," said Susan dreamily.

"Maybe," said Molly. "It's going to be so much fun!"

"Will you two come on?" said Linda. She led the way to the house.

The three girls raced inside, through the warm, bright kitchen, and down the stairs to the basement. Their new hideaway was in the corner next to Dad's workbench. They had set up a card table there and draped an old blanket over it. It was their pretend bomb shelter. A few Saturdays ago, when they went to the movies, they saw a newsreel that showed the different kinds of bomb shelters people used in England. One bomb shelter was a steel table with sides that rolled down. The sides were made of metal links. The table was set up in a living room. The newsreel showed a family rushing to get under the table at the sound of a warning siren. It seemed almost like a game, the same idea as musical chairs.

The girls had been very impressed. Imagine having a bomb shelter right in your own living room! It was horrifying and exciting at the same time. They had gone straight to Molly's house after the movies and made a pretend bomb shelter. They liked to sit under the blanket-covered table and play that the house was collapsing around them. It was pleasantly scary.

"It smells like mothballs in here," complained Linda as she crawled under the table. "Do we have to have this old blanket over the table all the time?"

"Yes!" said Molly. "Don't you remember the news-reel? When the bombs came, the people got under the table and rolled the sides down so they wouldn't get hurt."

"But those sides were like a fence," said Linda. "They had holes so you could at least breathe."

"Well, a blanket is the best we can do," said Molly. "Let's just play."

"Maybe the English girl has a bomb shelter just like this in her house in England," said Susan as she twisted the top off Molly's Girl Scout canteen. They kept the canteen full of water in case they decided to stay in their shelter for a long time. They wanted to keep crackers there, too, but Mrs. Gilford thought cracker crumbs would bring ants.

"Do you think English people ever stay in bomb shelters overnight?" asked Linda. "It's so crowded in here."

"I think sometimes they do," said Molly. She tried to straighten her legs, but there wasn't enough room under the table. "They have to stay in as long as the bombing goes on. Because if they came out too soon, something might fall on them, like bricks or—"

WHAM! Something heavy landed right above their heads. The table wobbled. BAM! The table was struck again.

"Bombs away!" they heard.

The girls looked at each other and giggled, "Ricky!"

Molly lifted the blanket and stuck her head out. Ricky was bouncing his basketball on top of the table. "Don't do that!" Molly said. She didn't mind very much, though, because the thud of the basketball made it very easy to pretend there were real bombs outside.

"Some bomb shelter," said Ricky. "This wouldn't last two seconds if a real bomb fell. Don't you girls know anything? Real bomb shelters are outside, dug into the ground like caves." He bounced the ball on the table again.

"This is like what they have in England," protested Molly.

"Like fish it is," scoffed Ricky.

"It is, too," said Susan from inside. "We saw it at the movies."

"Where? In the cartoon?" asked Ricky.

"You wait, Ricky," said Molly. "Wait till the English girl comes. She'll tell you about bomb shelters."

Ricky groaned. "Just what I need. Another dippy girl around." But Molly noticed he didn't say anything more about their bomb shelter.

Ricky had just left when Molly's mother called down the stairs. "Girls? Come up here, please."

"She's here!" squealed Molly. "The English girl!" The three girls tumbled over one another struggling to be the first one out of their bomb shelter. They pounded up the stairs and into the kitchen. Molly stopped so suddenly that Susan stumbled into her back.

There, standing by the kitchen table, was the English girl.

About the Author

VALERIE TRIPP says that she became a writer because of the kind of person she is. She says she's curious, and writing requires you to be interested in everything. Talking is her favorite sport, and writing is a way of talking on paper. She's a day-dreamer which helps her come up with ideas. And she loves words. She even loves the struggle to come up with the right words as she writes and rewrites. Ms. Tripp lives in Maryland with her husband.